Beautiful Forevers

Blueberry Beach Book Three

Jessie Gussman

Published By: Jessie Gussman

Contents

Acknowledgments

Cover art by Julia Gussman
Editing by Heather Hayden
Narration by Jay Dyess
Author Services by CE Author Assistant

Listen to a FREE professionally performed and produced audiobook version of this title on Youtube. Search for "Say With Jay" to browse all available FREE Dyess/Gussman audiobooks.

Chapter 1

Zoriah turned down the main street of Blueberry Beach, Michigan. Her niece, Macy, sat in the back, along with Macy's brother, Mark.

Zoriah still hadn't quite adjusted to looking into her rearview mirror and seeing that she wasn't alone in her car.

While she'd certainly spent time with her niece and nephew over the years, and especially in the last six months as her sister battled various health problems and rapidly advancing multiple sclerosis, they'd spent more time together in the last four weeks than they had in her entire life.

They'd all been through a funeral and a burial, and this was the kids' second move. The first one from their house to Zoriah's, and now the second one from Kankakee in southern Ohio to Blueberry Beach.

Her grandma's shop was along Main Street. It almost felt like coming home as she drove down the mostly deserted street, except Gram had passed away two years ago, and while things felt familiar, nothing would ever be the same.

It was only April. Tourist season in Blueberry Beach wouldn't get underway for real for another two months.

There was plenty of time for her to open her grandmother's old clothing and apparel shop and figure out the ins and outs of owning her own business.

A girl on rollerblades flew by in the middle of the street while another girl rolled toward her backwards.

Maybe some people would be irritated at having to slow down to keep from hitting them, but the sight made Zoriah smile.

Blueberry Beach was that kind of town—the kind of town kids could roller-skate down the street in—nine months out of the year at least.

As Zoriah remembered it, life was slow and happy and the community close knit and helpful.

After her grandmother's death, Zoriah had inherited the building, and until the death of her sister, Zoriah hadn't been sure what she was going to do with the shop.

She was committed now.

Her house had been sold, and she left her job as an LPN at a local doctor's office in Kankakee.

"We're here," she said, glancing in the rearview before pulling into the parking place directly in front of her grandmother's shop.

The windows were bare, dusty, and dirty, and the place didn't look nearly as warm and welcoming as it did in her memories.

She supposed nothing ever was exactly the way a person remembered it. Now, it was up to her to make it warm and welcoming.

Some of the same old shops lined both sides of the streets, while she saw a couple of new signs out as well.

She didn't recognize the ice-cream and candy store, although it was in the same place as the candy store had been before.

She didn't recall it having ice cream, and the sign was different.

But the diner was still there, and the surf shop, and there were still bikes sitting out in a rack along the sidewalk with a big for rent sign on them.

She shut the car off and pushed her door open. The day was breezy and warm, a little warmer than typical for Michigan in April, but she wasn't complaining about the warmth.

Michiganders never did.

She was back where she'd spent every summer of her growing-up years and loved it.

A lot of loss. A lot of heartbreak in the last three years, and not just for her.

She watched as Macy got out of the car, her earbuds still plugged in her ears, her eyes scanning the town.

Her niece and nephew had been hit even harder than she over their family's losses.

God might shut the door, but He always opens a window.

She wasn't sure that was Bible, but it seemed to be a truth that a lot of people lived by. Hopefully, it would be true in her life as well, even if God did seem to be taking His good old time about getting that window open.

Maybe it was stuck.

"Those people were skating on the street!" Mark said, pointing as the same blonde teen Zoriah had slowed down for flew by them. Her face was wreathed in a smile, and she waved, which startled Zoriah—she'd forgotten that everyone waved to everyone in small towns—and the girl wasn't looking anymore when she pulled herself together and got her hand up to wave back.

Kankakee, the small city she lived in in Ohio, hadn't been huge, but they weren't friendly like Blueberry Beach.

"Did you know her?" Macy asked, turning big brown eyes to Zoriah.

"No. That's just the way people are in small towns. They wave at everyone."

"Everyone?" Macy asked with disbelief in her voice.

"And they skate in the street, too," Mark said, more than a little eagerness in his voice.

As far as Zoriah knew, he didn't have any skates, but the longing on his face said that he wished he did.

She hadn't gone through all of their stuff. They'd been old enough to pack most of it themselves. What they hadn't taken from their house in Kankakee, she'd placed in storage.

"Can I get a pair of skates?" Mark asked, confirming her suspicions.

Her bank account wasn't quite at zero, but she only had two more checks coming from her job before they dried up, and she had no income until the store was open and running.

The inventory had been ordered, and she'd had to pay for it before they would fill it, so she didn't have to worry about that at least.

There were plenty of other things to worry about instead.

She bit her lip, hating to tell her nephew no.

Becoming a guardian to Macy had been easy, and she had a great rapport with her. Macy had been president of Girls for Jesus at her old high school. She also taught the Peewee class of Girls for Jesus at the local elementary school. She was on the student council, captain of her hockey team, and an award-winning member of their debate team.

Macy was the perfect student, the perfect daughter, the perfect niece.

She made Zoriah feel incompetent at times, but thankfully, she didn't seem to need Zoriah's help much and had seemed to bounce back from her mother's death with no problems.

Mark was a completely different story. She didn't feel as secure with Mark, maybe because she'd never been around teen boys much, and she'd really like to say yes to his request, but she couldn't afford to shell out that kind of money right now.

"Once I get the shop open and running, I'll think about it. But until then, I don't want to buy anything that's not essential."

Mark wrinkled his nose and pushed his lower lip out. It wasn't hard to see that he thought she was being mean on purpose, and while she didn't think that Mark would actually do anything illegal, she hoped he wouldn't get involved with the wrong crowd, possibly as a retaliation for everything that had gone wrong in his life so far.

She knew kids who had completely turned away from their upbringing after some big traumatic event in their life.

Mark had had more than just one big traumatic event.

It was always so disappointing to see that happen to children who had grown up in the pediatric practice where she'd worked—kids she'd given immunizations to, children she'd seen for the flu and sinus infections, earaches and stitches, then, before she knew it, they were taller than her, and their parents were in with their little brothers and sisters and crying because their child had made terrible choices and now had a juvie record.

She and the other office personnel talked about them during lunch breaks, with sadness and hurting hearts, as they wondered how good kids from solid families who had been given so much could throw everything away.

As much as she was able, she wouldn't let that happen to Mark.

Still, she wasn't going to be able to swing for a pair of rollerblades. Hopefully, that wouldn't be the deciding factor in his life of crime.

She hit the lever and popped the trunk of her small car, saying to her niece and nephew, "Grab your stuff out of the back. We're gonna go on in and see what the place looks like."

Maybe she should have come and checked the place out before she sold her home and moved her niece and nephew across two states.

As far as she knew, the furniture that her grandmother had left was all still in the building. She'd come out two years ago when she inherited it, closed everything up after cleaning, and hadn't been back. She'd been taking care of her sister at the time, since it was after her parents had died in the hit-and-run.

Her stomach cramped, and she stood with her door open, her hand on it, feeling like she was making a terrible mistake.

It all seemed so simple and easy and the best thing for everyone when she'd been thinking about it back in Ohio.

Now that she was actually here, she was scared out of her wits.

What did she know about running an apparel store?

Other than working behind the counter and stocking shelves with her grandma when she was younger. She'd never actually had to pay any of the bills or order anything or do any of the other things that were involved in running a business.

She'd had some help from her accountant and was pretty sure she was good with all the tax stuff, which she never could have figured out on her own.

It was all so complicated.

Who knew the government had such detailed and exacting regulations?

When people talked about simplifying the tax code, she'd had no idea it was that complicated.

Shaking her head, trying to push the worrying thoughts aside—surely the IRS wouldn't jail her if she didn't know what she was doing?—she went to shut her door, but her hand was sweating from her attack of nerves, and it slipped off. She stumbled backwards.

She hadn't even seen the man coming on the rollerblades until he crashed into her hard enough to send her sprawling. She skidded into a painful heap on the warm blacktop. A man came down behind her, managing to fly over her and land shoulder first beyond her, the velocity of his movement making him roll twice before he came to a stop with a groan.

Zoriah wasn't quite sure whether the apology was her responsibility or his, and that thought kind of swirled around in the mucky mess that her brain had become.

Pain from her elbow, pain from her ankle, and a burning sensation crept down her arm.

She realized that both her niece and nephew were fine as they bent over her and that the man was at least alive as he grunted. The girls that had been skating with him came to a stop beside him.

"Dad? Are you okay?" a soft voice said. Not one she recognized. Not her niece or nephew.

Of course, they didn't typically call her "Dad," and in a more coherent time, she would have noticed that right away, instead of having to think about it.

She closed her eyes, trying to lift her lips into a little smile to let them know she was fine.

The man spoke to the girl who asked the question, but she didn't hear because Macy was speaking at the same time. "Aunt Zoriah? Did you pass out?"

Her head wobbled back and forth, and pain shot across her forehead.

Had she hit her head when she fell?

She didn't think so. That at least didn't seem to hurt, not the back of her head anyway. It was the front that felt a headache coming on.

"No. I just need a few moments," she said weakly, hating the fact that her voice wobbled. She didn't want to be weak, not right now. Mark and Macy needed her to be strong, and she had every intention in the world of being that for them.

Except, right now, she felt anything but.

At least she wasn't worried about whether or not she was making the right decision to move.

She was more concerned about whether or not she'd broken any bones.

She should have been paying better attention. It was her fault they'd fallen. Wasn't it?

Chapter 2

Gage lay on the ground and gingerly wiggled each finger before bending his wrist then his elbows.

He thought he'd landed oddly before rolling, and pain shot up his arm, but nothing seemed to be broken.

He shouldn't have turned around to talk to Naomi.

He knew better, but he'd just been going to tell her that he was going to stop and she could go on without him, since she needed to be behind the candy store counter in fifteen minutes.

They'd been having so much fun he'd lost track of time.

He hadn't gotten any of that out of his mouth though, because when he turned around to glance at his daughter, he must have shifted direction just a little and plowed smack into the brown-haired woman who was parked in front of Grandma Heater's old clothing store.

His girls had grown up loving Grandma Heater, trying jewelry and clothes on in the back room on lazy winter afternoons as the snow blew in off Lake Michigan and he was on a conference call or something else that he could hardly do with two daughters running around his apartment.

Working from home was great until one needed the privacy that an office typically afforded but a home usually didn't.

Grandma Heater had always been not just willing but eager to watch his kids.

When she couldn't do it, Iva May who worked at the diner would have been willing to watch them for a bit.

That was one of the really great things about living in Blueberry Beach. Everyone helped everyone else, which is what led to the dilemma he found himself in now.

He had been going to stop and ask this lady if he could do something to help her.

She was parked in front of Grandma Heater's, which made him think that she was going shopping, but when the kids started lifting bags out of the back of the car, he thought maybe something else was going on, and he could give them a hand.

He hadn't meant to give a body slam.

He had to work on his presentation there, he supposed.

Grunting, because even if his arm wasn't broken, his wrist hurt pretty bad—it was at least sprained—he managed to push up to a sitting position and look over the lady that he had practically decapitated.

"I promise that wasn't a botched suicide mission," he said, realizing his first words should have been asking her if she were okay but hoping the woman had a sense of humor.

That would make the next few minutes a lot less awkward.

She took a breath and pushed up, nodding shakily. "Thank you for the reassurance. I was hoping that Blueberry Beach hadn't changed that much since my grandmother passed away."

Gage blinked, clearing his eyesight.

"Zoriah?" he asked, trying to recognize the woman that he'd met several times at Grandma Heater's store in the lady that he'd practically run over.

At the sound of her name, her head lifted, and her eyes squinted. "Gage?"

He grinned. He didn't know her well, but he'd met her several times, and with a name like Zoriah, he could hardly forget her.

"It's me," he said, feeling stupid, but happy that she was at least speaking despite the fact that they'd both had a pretty big fall.

"Did I do something to you the last time we spoke?" she asked with a tilted lift to her brow and her lips lopsided.

He hadn't thought of her as someone who was terribly funny, but thankfully, she did seem to have a well-developed sense of humor.

"I really am sorry. I was actually going to stop and help you."

"That was a little more help than what I was thinking I needed," she said with more than a little irony in her voice.

He laughed. "I was telling my daughter that she could go ahead and get ready for work…" He looked around. Naomi was bent down on her haunches looking at him with Lexi on the other side.

"I'm fine, girls. I know you have to be behind the counter at the candy store, Naomi. I've got this."

"Sierra texted me, and she wanted to know if I could take her shift this afternoon. So I need to go too, Daddy. Are you sure you're okay?" Lexi said, her brows crinkled, but she was throwing interested glances at the teenage girl who was standing overtop of Zoriah.

Or maybe those glances were going to the boy. He looked young to Gage, but then, the older he got, the younger everyone looked.

"Super cool!" the girl kneeling beside Zoriah said. "You work in a candy store?"

She seemed really friendly and sweet. Not pushy, but her smile was just that kind of expression that made a person trust her almost immediately.

Naomi wasn't shy, but this girl seemed even more outgoing.

"I do. And the owners are super nice. I'm sure if you wanted to, you could come over and check it out. They're looking to hire at least one more employee for the summer. If you're looking for a job, they might think about hiring you."

"I hadn't even thought about it, but definitely. If it's okay with you, Aunt Zoriah?"

He noticed the terminology: aunt.

He hadn't thought about Zoriah's marital status since she was never a permanent fixture. The few times they met, she'd been coming or going. He hadn't been in town when she'd been growing up.

The word "aunt," though, made him drop his eyes. Her finger was bare.

"Would that be okay?" Zoriah asked, looking first at Naomi and then at Gage.

Both his girls were already nodding. "Adam and Lindy Coates own the store. They're good friends of mine and well-known in the community. They won't mind at all, as long as the girls are mature and responsible. Which I'm sure they will be." He added that last part to ease the sting of what was a thinly veiled command.

His daughters were usually very good, but they weren't perfect. Naomi and he had butted heads some, but his girls were pretty good kids.

The girls chattered as they walked away, leaving Zoriah and him still sitting, facing each other on the sidewalk, along with the boy, who had straightened from his hunched position when the girls did but stayed where he was, taking his sister's backpack, which she had thrust at him before she left.

"I hope that was okay," Gage said, realizing they had just gotten into town and maybe she had plans.

"It's fine. I had been concerned about moving her. There's been a lot going on. I'm glad to see she has some friends, and so quickly. And close." She took another breath, as though still recovering from her accident, and then said, "Are you still living above the store across the street?"

She lifted her chin in the direction of his apartment, and Gage nodded. He'd been living there for years. "I remember your gram saying you grew up in Blueberry Beach, is that right?"

She nodded, and they both started climbing gingerly to their feet.

"That's not fair that Macy gets to go play with friends. Why do I have to hold her bag and help you unpack?" the boy said with a definite whine in his voice.

It wasn't hard for Gage to remember what it was like to be a young boy, and if there was anything worse than other kids playing, especially a sibling, while he had to work, Gage couldn't remember what it was. Unless it was missing a meal.

Gage wondered how Zoriah was going to handle that. Sibling rivalry and jealousy, a common issue with parenting when one had more than one child.

Only children presented their own issues, he supposed.

More than once, his daughters had been upset because one got to do something that the other one didn't.

Now that they were older, it wasn't quite as bad.

Zoriah seemed to ignore her nephew's question, though, and pulled a set of keys out of her pocket. "Mark, would you mind taking these and seeing if one of them will unlock the door? It's been years since I've opened it. I think the key is on there, but I don't remember which one it is."

At the sight of the keys and the responsibility that implied, Mark's eyes lit up.

It wouldn't settle the sibling issue, but it would distract him for a while.

Gage cleared his throat, abashed that he had made things harder for her. "I was going to offer to help you." He realized he should quit talking about it and just do it. "Is there something I can do to help you?" He paused with a little self-effacing grin. "If I promise that I'll try not to run into you again?"

She huffed a laugh, like he was kind of hoping she would.

"No hard feelings?" he asked. Although he thought he knew the answer since she was laughing at his weak jokes.

"Of course not. It was an accident and just as much my fault as yours. I should have been looking where I was going instead of getting out of the car entertaining old memories."

"I think we must have missed each other. I've lived here for more than ten years, moving here right after my divorce." He couldn't help it. His words softened a little at the end of that sentence.

Even now, the thought of his divorce made him sad. Not necessarily because he missed his wife, although on one level, he supposed he did. Just because raising two girls alone was hard, not necessarily because he missed the fighting and the insults and the constant mind games she played.

He shook that off.

"And if I recall correctly from the few times your grandmother introduced us, you grew up here?"

She nodded. "My parents were in and out of my life. My grandma was really the only stability I had. So yeah, I spent most of my time here, although I did move around some with my parents. My sister and I."

"Oh. I don't think I've ever met your sister?"

"That's Macy and Mark's mother. She passed away a month ago."

"I'm so sorry."

Her eyes turned down, and she stuck her tongue out and touched her top lip, as though the memories upset her.

"I'm sorry. I didn't mean to bring up the past. You lost your grandmother and your sister. That must be hard."

"My parents were killed in a car accident not long before my sister died. It's not just me though. Macy and Mark have been through it all too. It's been a pretty long, tough stretch of death and dying and funerals. I'm ready to come here and just sink into the beach vibe, the summer fun, and the memories I have of the close-knit community and all the good times I used to have here."

"It's a wonderful town. Safe." He chuckled a little. "Quiet enough that you can roller-skate down the street, although not quiet enough that you can get out of your car without being tackled by said roller skater."

They laughed together, and then he held out his hands, as though reminding her of his question. He didn't want to push, and if she didn't want his help, he didn't want to insist on it.

"If you don't mind, we do have some bags that need to be carried out."

"The key works! It's this one! The blue one." Mark, holding up what Gage assumed to be the blue key, had turned around from the door and walked across the sidewalk, standing on the other side of the car. "Two years don't make a difference, since the door opened right up. It stinks in there though." He wiggled his nose.

Maybe Zoriah was tempted to correct Mark's language, but she didn't. Instead, she smiled. "Thank you so much! I just couldn't remember which one it was. All of those keys work somewhere around here. As I recall, there's a cellar door that locks, and there's a key for our apartment in the back, and a key for the door for the apartment that runs through the shop. We need to figure them out and maybe mark them or just decide how we can remember them so we don't have to go through every key on the ring in order to get the right one."

Mark grinned, his chest seeming to puff out even more, and he said, "If it's okay, I'll do that right now."

"Hang on a second." Zoriah pulled her purse off her shoulder and started digging in it. "I think I have a permanent marker in here, and you can at least initial the keys unless you think of a better way to mark them?" She quieted as she pulled the marker out of her purse and held it over the car.

Mark grabbed it, and his expression was confident. "I'll use this. Maybe some tape or something would work, but this will work just fine for now. Except, this is the only blue key on the ring. So it'll be easy to remember. It's the front door to the store."

He held the ring of keys up again as he spoke, and then he turned around and started walking toward the door again.

Almost as though he wanted to check to be sure, he stopped and looked back. "Did you say it was okay if I did this now?"

"Yes. Mr. Gage said he would help me carry things up, so you can get the keys squared away right now."

"All right!" Mark said, going to the door and disappearing inside the shop.

Zoriah bit her lip. "Maybe I should have told him to be careful. I haven't been here in two years. Surely everything is okay?"

"I'm sure it is. Plus, the kid looks like he's old enough to take care of himself, and a little adventure is good for a guy at any age," Gage said, although he probably really didn't mean it. When was the last time he had any kind of adventure beyond roller-skating down the street?

Chapter 3

Zoriah truly appreciated Gage's offer to help. He didn't seem put out by it, either. Maybe he was making up for knocking her down. Her arm still burned, and she thought when she looked at it that she might have a small stone or two stuck in the brush burn.

Not enough to make a big deal about.

Gage's offer of help allowed her to give Mark something to make up for the fact that she'd allowed Macy to leave and she wouldn't be helping them. One more parenting mistake in what had become a long list of them since her sister had passed away.

In hindsight, Zoriah shouldn't have allowed Macy to go until they had the car unloaded.

She wasn't used to being a mom, and she was making a terrible one.

Pointing out the box full of spices and kitchen items and another box with paper products in it, she waited while Gage lifted the boxes she indicated before she grabbed bags for herself that contained fresh bed linens and towels.

"I really appreciate you helping me. I do think sometimes Mark gets frustrated because Macy always seems to land on her feet, making friends and always having something to do, while he works a little harder for it."

Gage nodded. "I understand. My girls are different too. The older one is more outgoing, and a lot of times, the younger one rides on her coattails. Maybe that's just the way families are?"

Zoriah nodded. "Each kid has their own strengths?"

"Yeah. Exactly. Sometimes, I think instead of appreciating our own strengths, we look at someone else and wish we had theirs. Where, in reality, God made us the way we are so we would be able to contribute using our own strengths."

"That's such a good point. I'd never considered that before. We spend so much time eyeing other people and wishing we could do what they do that we don't realize that we're not doing what God made us to do."

Zoriah had figured that the tingling sensation in her stomach was somehow related to the fall that she taken or maybe just being in close proximity to a handsome man. But a conversation with substance, one that challenged her and made her think, especially with a man, was rare.

She eyed Gage with renewed interest as she followed him to the front door.

She hadn't come to Blueberry Beach for romance.

"I'll get the door," she said, since she was carrying bags with handles and could set them down on the sidewalk.

"I've got it." He maneuvered the boxes so his hand stuck out, and he grabbed the doorknob, holding it open and allowing her to go first.

She smiled and murmured thank you, and reminded herself that her niece and nephew came first. Maybe it was irony that she had given up ever getting married and determined to put her life on the back burner while she took care of her sister's children.

If today was any indication, Gage would be a temptation for her.

Maybe she wouldn't have anything to worry about since she might not be a temptation for him.

"I already told you I was divorced. You mentioned Macy and Mark are your sister's children. Don't you have any?"

That seemed like a personal question. One she might not answer for just anyone.

But Gage had been in Blueberry Beach for a decade or more, and her grandma had always spoken very highly of him. He was the kind of man that she'd be interested in, if she were interested. Which, she had to remind herself, she wasn't.

"I had a couple of long-term relationships back in my twenties and into my thirties. Two. Each time, I thought they were going to lead to more, and had I known they wouldn't, I wouldn't have invested nearly as much time and effort into them as I did."

She sighed. She hadn't expected her life would turn out the way it had. Single in her mid-forties with no family, other than her sister and her parents, who were now gone. Of course, there was her niece and nephew, who were now her responsibility. It sometimes felt overwhelming.

She walked ahead of him into the dim interior of the store. After her grandmother died, she'd had several weeks of sales, with everything deeply discounted, and there was just one rack of odds and ends of clothing left. Otherwise, the room was dim and empty other than dusty clothes racks and the counter where the old-fashioned cash register still sat.

It probably still worked. It wasn't even electronic.

"I guess I never answered you, did I?" she said as she waited for Gage to catch up to her. It took a little while for her eyes to adjust to the dimness of the hallway, since the light from the windows didn't reach back that far.

"I suppose I could read between the lines. You were never married, and you don't have children. And you kind of regret it."

Her eyes widened, and she turned away, walking down the hall even though she couldn't see.

He definitely read her like a book, and she hadn't intended for that.

Mark was right. The room did stink. But underneath the stench of musty dust and disuse, she could just catch a whiff of her grandmother's perfume.

Her throat tightened, and her stomach felt stiff and full.

The backs of her eyeballs itched, and she wanted to sit down and wrap her arms around her waist and mourn for her family.

Her grandmother, her dad, her mom, her sister. All the people she grew up with. Gone. Mark and Macy were all she had left, and sometimes she wondered if she might be holding on to them too tightly. They were teens, wanting to grow and stretch their wings, and she was middle-aged, getting older every day, and just wanting to keep her family close to her.

"You're right. You're right." She said the second phrase softer as she went through the door that Mark had apparently left open and started climbing the staircase, which, as was typical of an older building, was narrow and rather rickety.

The banister wiggled, and she said over her shoulder, "Please be careful. The banister is more wobbly than I remember. Although Gram always told me not to slide down it, not because she loved her banister, but because she loved her granddaughter."

Gage chuckled behind her. "Your grandmother was quite a woman," he said. "I don't know anyone who didn't admire her."

"Me either," Zoriah said, and she worked hard to keep the sadness out of her voice.

Gage had already figured her out more than she wanted him to. She didn't want to be a pathetic person with no family and only sadness in her heart and life. She could smile and she could be happy, and she wouldn't let the sadness win.

"Aunt Zoriah, I found the bedroom that I want! Since Macy isn't here, I get to choose, right?" Mark's voice came from the top of the stairs.

Zoriah thought that seemed like a fair idea. But she'd also figured out in the last month that she couldn't just go with her first instinct. Sometimes, it was dead wrong.

She said, "Let's think about that."

She couldn't think of a reason why he couldn't pick his bedroom, and then Macy could pick from the other two.

"I want this one because the walls are blue. One of the others has pink walls and I don't want the one that's left because it has flowers around the ceiling. They're pink, too. I know Macy hates pink, but I'm a boy. So, I guess she's just stuck with it."

"Maybe we can paint the walls," she said, although she had a hard time injecting enthusiasm into that.

"Not a painter?" Gage spoke behind her as he walked up the staircase.

She pulled out one of the old metal chairs with the plastic cushions with her foot and set one of the bags she carried down on it. The other plopped down on the floor before she turned.

"That obvious?" She exchanged a smile with him, because she hadn't meant to be so see-through. Maybe she should pay more attention to how she was coming off. Maybe all of the grief and sorrow she'd been through had suddenly made her start wearing her emotions on her sleeves.

"Yeah. Sorry, but it was," he said with a grin. "But you have a neighbor across the street who actually specializes in painting as a stress relief from his day job, which mostly involves sitting in front of a computer running numbers and occasionally having Zoom calls with people who are just as boring as I am."

"You're not boring," Zoriah said automatically. She almost accepted his offer on the spot, then she bit her lip and looked away. Her shrinking bank account loomed large.

Almost as though Gage knew exactly why she looked away, he said, "And when I said neighbor, I meant neighbor. I wasn't asking you to hire me as a handyman."

"Oh! I couldn't ask you to do that."

"You didn't ask. I offered. And I meant it. I've repainted my own apartment three different times. The entire thing. My girls will attest to that fact."

He walked forward and set the boxes on the table.

"In fact, they would probably be relieved if I were painting someone else's apartment instead of our own. They've both expressed their desire to be able to live in our apartment and not have drop rags and paint rollers and masking tape spread out everywhere."

He grinned, an endearing grin that would probably get her to say yes to playing outside underneath an oak tree in a lightning storm.

Which is why she should say no.

"Well, maybe my own family won't be very happy with that."

"Macy will. She hates pink, and she'd do anything to keep from having to stay in a room with walls that color. Aunt Zoriah, they're not just pink, they're *really* pink."

"I remember. That room is such a happy room," Zoriah said, remembering as a child how much she loved the color, and then as she got into her teen years, how she'd thought that her grandmother had no taste at all, and then as she'd gotten even older, she'd looked at the walls with new eyes and just thought they seemed happy and cheerful and the perfect kind of walls to look at during the long Michigan winter.

Funny how a person's perspective changed as they aged.

If only she could have been as wise when she was younger as she felt now. Although, there were also days where she felt like she knew nothing. Absolutely nothing.

"So maybe you want to leave the walls the color they are? That's fine," Gage said as he stepped back away from the table.

"The whole apartment could use sprucing up," she said, as much as she didn't want to. She didn't want to change anything that had been her grandmother's, not to mention she didn't want to owe Gage.

But that was unfair to Macy and Mark and wasn't the way she wanted to live her life, stuck in the past. They were going to live here. They needed to make it their own.

But that didn't mean taking advantage of the neighbor's kindness. "I don't want you to feel like you have to, no matter what we decide."

"My offer stands. I'm dead serious about loving painting. Although I do have a full-time job, and it won't be like I'll be in here two days and the entire apartment will be painted." He stood, shoving his hands in his pockets and looking around. "I've never been up here, and I'm not sure how big it is, but if there are three bedrooms, plus this kitchen, and that looks like a living room in there. The bathroom, I assume... At least a month, and that will be a month in the winter, not in the summer when everything's busy and the kids are home from school."

She nodded. "No. If you are doing my work and I'm not paying you for it, I wouldn't expect you to do it within a certain amount of time." But then she felt like she needed to add, "Although, I wouldn't want to drag it out for years, either."

He smiled that slow grin again, and her stomach did that odd buzzing that made her backbone vibrate. "That's reasonable. More than two days, less than a year. I can work in that timeframe."

She chuckled, shaking her head and looking around at the walls.

Mark had disappeared in the bedrooms again, probably looking at the nooks and crannies. A couple of them were interestingly shaped, and most of her grandmother's furniture was still in them.

"I suppose it's terrible that I don't want to change anything because it almost feels like a betrayal of my grandmother."

"I get it. But you have to make it yours, too."

"I thought that, too." She sighed. She couldn't live in the past.

"You know, I lost my wife. In the divorce. It's not like she died, but it took me a long time to realize she'd be with me forever. In my memories and the memories of my kids and in the faces and actions of my children. I had to see it as a beautiful forever and not want to live in the past. Or I think the opposite of that is to cut the past out of my life. I can't do either one of those things. I have to come to grips with the past and live with it in the present, seeing the beauty and overlooking the ugly parts."

Zoriah's eyes flew to his, and she couldn't help it; hers were wide.

She'd spent thirty minutes with this man, and twice now, he had astounded her by telling her things that she really should have known herself but that were so deep and true. And despite all the people she talked to and all the time that she'd spent getting over the deaths of her family, she'd never thought of the things he'd said.

"I'm so glad you're my neighbor. I'm glad you'll be here painting. Talking to you today has been one of the best things that has happened to me," she said, meaning every word.

"It's funny how the Lord brings things in our life at just the right time."

Their eyes met. Maybe he was saying more than what she was hearing, or maybe he was thinking something totally different. All she knew was she was having trouble pulling her eyes away, and they stood there in her grandmother's kitchen, staring at each other.

"Aunt Zoriah?" Mark came out and interrupted them.

"Yes?" she said, swallowing and blinking and trying to get her bearings again.

"If Mr. Gage is going to paint, can I help him?"

She lifted her brows and looked back at Gage.

"Of course. I try to get my girls to help me, but for some reason, they'd rather hang out down in the candy shop or play in the beach band. I'd love to have help."

"Cool! Then Macy can pick a room, and if I end up with the pink room, we'll paint the walls. If I don't have to have pink, I'll take any room."

"Wow. That's so nice of you," Zoriah said. "I'm sure Macy will care, and it's awfully big of you to step back and allow someone else to have first choice, especially when it probably should be you who gets to choose."

Mark grinned, and his shoulders seemed to go back.

Still, he was hurting, even if he was the one who probably showed it the least.

She just hoped she had what the kids needed. The grief counselor at their old church had recommended someone from a church in this town, and she supposed she should call them as soon as Gage left. She wanted the children to be able to get through this and use it as a positive in their life. A positive, beautiful forever.

Was that even possible?

Chapter 4

Zoriah spent the day cleaning. When Gage left, Zoriah had asked him to send Macy back over, and Macy and Mark had reluctantly helped her.

She'd been able to clean the bed linens, figure out which kid was going to be in which bedroom, and thoroughly scrub the kitchen.

By suppertime, she was exhausted, and knowing that she still had more apartment to clean plus she had to have the downstairs area clean and ready for her delivery in the next week, she decided to go to the diner for supper.

It didn't used to be open in the evening, but she'd sent Mark out to check the door to see what the hours were.

When he'd announced it didn't close until seven, she'd made sure she left by 5:30.

She tried not to think about her bank account, and she also needed to put grocery shopping on her list of things to do as well as making a meal for tomorrow so she wouldn't end up eating out again.

It was a lot more expensive for three people to eat out than it was for just one.

All the things that she was learning—slowly—as she got used to having kids.

As she was grabbing her purse and waiting for the kids to go down the steps before her, she thought they must be having just as much trouble getting used to her.

Although sometimes, kids could be more resilient than adults.

So, after they walked out of the shop door, and she locked it behind them, giving the key to Mark and loving the proud smile on his face as he put the ring in his pocket, pleased that he was the man of the family, she asked, "I know we talked about moving here, and I asked you guys what you thought. But I was thinking today as I was cleaning that getting used to me must be pretty hard for you. Is there anything I can do to make it easier?"

Macy was on one side of her, Mark on the other. Neither one of them looked at her, with Mark looking at the ground and Macy stretching out her hand and looking at her fingernails.

Maybe kids just didn't think like that. Or maybe they didn't want to talk about their mother.

They walked in silence for a little bit before Mark finally said, "I guess I don't think about it until you do something differently than what I know my mom would. And then that makes me miss her."

Why had she wanted to have this conversation? His words hurt, and they also made her sad.

"But sometimes you do things that are exactly the same as Mom, and it makes me smile. And I guess we just have to get used to new things. Some of the things you do are better." He added that last bit kind of casually with a lifted shoulder. It didn't erase all the sad feelings, but it made her feel a lot better.

Maybe there wasn't any right way to navigate this. Maybe there were a lot of different right ways, but there probably were also a lot of different wrong ways as well.

"You're doing just fine, Aunt Zoriah," Macy said, slipping her arm in through Zoriah's. "You loved Mom just like we did. Sometimes, when I wish things were back the way they used to be, before Mom got sick, I think that your life isn't the same either."

That seemed kind of deep coming from a teenager.

Zoriah put her hand over top of Macy's hand on her arm and squeezed. "Thank you. It takes a mature person to look beyond yourself and think about how someone else might feel. That's actually more than a lot of adults do sometimes."

She certainly had been a lot more selfish when she was Macy's age.

Of course, her family had been kind of scattered but not dead.

They reached the diner door, and Mark hurried around, pulling it open and waiting for them to walk through.

Macy walked in without saying anything.

Zoriah figured now wasn't the time, but later she needed to make sure she reminded Macy that even though Mark was doing what he was told to do, she needed to thank him.

Gratefulness might be a hard sell for two children who had lost their mother, a dad who had never really been there, their grandparents, and their great-grandmother, and had no one in the world other than an aunt who had no clue of how to raise them.

Or maybe not. Maybe all that would help them be thankful for what they had, since they knew how easily things could be lost. Forever.

Which reminded her of what Gage had said about the beautiful forevers.

She supposed beautiful forevers were better than ugly or terrible forevers.

The diner was seat yourself, and the kids had already started walking toward a booth by the windows, so she put that out of her mind. It was something she wanted to consider later.

"This is different. We used to walk to the counter and order, but it looks like you seat yourself now and there's a waitress."

It had been a long time since she'd been in the diner, but she was sure that was the way it was. She remembered standing at the diner counter and ordering her first cappuccino. It seemed so exotic at the time, and now almost thirty years later, she'd had countless cappuccinos, and they weren't any big deal.

Back then, she would not have given a flip about beautiful forevers, and now her perspective had totally shifted.

An older lady walked over and stood beside their table. "Can I get you all some drinks?"

"Iva May?"

Iva May's eyes lifted from her pad and narrowed, searching over Zoriah's face.

Suddenly, recognition flashed in her eyes. "You're Grandma Heater's granddaughter!"

"I am. Zoriah."

"Well, I'll be. It's been years," Iva May said, turning and calling over her shoulder, "Anitra! Anitra! Guess who's here?"

Anitra had been a lot younger than Zoriah had been growing up in Blueberry Beach, but they'd still been casual friends.

Zoriah wasn't sure she would recognize the woman coming toward her as the young girl that had been friends with her.

She was carrying a baby, and her face just beamed.

"Oh my goodness...Zoriah? Is that you?"

Zoriah stood, putting one arm around Anitra in a hug and squeezing tight before pulling back just a little. "You have a little one?"

"I do. Wren," she said with a smile.

"She's so adorable!" Zoriah touched the little baby fist. "Where's Jordan?" She looked around, asking about Anitra's son that Zoriah had met when he was a toddler and seen several times over the years.

Anitra's face fell, and Zoriah immediately tightened the arm that was around her in concern. "He passed away last year. His cancer came back."

"Oh no! I'm so sorry to hear that!" Zoriah said, remembering that Jordan had had cancer, but the last that she'd heard, before her grandmother had passed away, was that he had beaten it. "With my grandmother gone, I just haven't heard anything."

Anitra shook her head and smiled softly. "Don't worry about it. Please. Of course, I'm sad that I don't have him with me here, but I honestly think everything worked out for the best." She looked at the little one in her arms. "If Jordan hadn't gotten sick, we might not have Wren, and not that one child replaces another, but God wanted to bless us with so many other things, we just had to let Him have Jordan first."

Beautiful forevers.

The thought went through Zoriah's mind again. Looking at something that was terrible and tragic—the death of a child—and seeing it as a positive. As a part of God's plan and how all of life worked together to provide those beautiful forevers.

"That's incredible," she finally said softly, and Anitra smiled.

"My husband is in the kitchen. He used to just be the breakfast shift, but sometimes, we tap him for lunch and dinner too."

"He came back?" Zoriah asked and had trouble keeping the shock out of her voice. The last she'd heard, Anitra's husband had been a deadbeat, and Anitra was better off without him. Still, going through the cancer of her child alone must have been really hard, and maybe it had brought him back.

"Oh no. Danny and I are divorced. But I met John because of Jordan's illness." There was that serene smile again and the complete confidence that her difficulties had proven worthwhile. "Let me go get him. I've told him all about you and the things we used to do when we were kids. I know he'd love to meet you."

"Oh no. You don't have to do that. I'll be around... I... I'm opening my grand-mother's shop." Somehow, saying it out loud made it real and very, very scary. "This is my niece and nephew."

Zoriah introduced Mark and Macy.

She chatted for a bit more, feeling even better about moving to Blueberry Beach. It felt like home even without her grandmother. Although her grand-mother's spirit, her touch, her scent, the things she had were still here, making it seem like Zoriah could walk into her at any time.

"I'll be back with your drinks," Iva May said. "It's so good to have you back," she added before she walked away.

After their food eventually arrived, Anitra came back, bringing John so she could introduce them.

He seemed like a really nice man, and Zoriah was so happy for Anitra who deserved someone kind and gentle after putting up with the man she'd been married to before.

Grandma Heater didn't have too many bad things to say about anyone, but Zoriah had never heard her say anything good about Anitra's first husband.

They finished eating, and Iva May brought their bill over.

"It's been so good to see you again," Zoriah had to say. Her heart was full, and she knew without a shadow of a doubt that she made the right decision moving her niece and nephew back to Blueberry Beach. It might not be perfect, but it was exactly where she needed to be. It was a perfect place to raise kids, even if Macy and Mark were already almost raised.

"I'm so happy to see you and to get to meet your niece and nephew." Iva May smiled at the teens. "Your great-grandmother talked so much about you before she passed away."

"Mom never talked about her much," Mark said, kind of mumbling.

"Well, sometime when you guys have time, you can come on over to my house. It's right back here, just a short walk from your shop. Straight back if you go out the back door of the diner. Anyway, you come on over, I'll pour you some tea, and I'll tell you all you want to know about your grandmother. She was a pretty amazing lady." Iva May's eyes twinkled, and her white hair seemed to glow.

"Maybe I could come too?" Zoriah almost put her hand over her mouth. Her grandmother would be giving her "that look" if she were still alive for inviting herself over to someone's house without an invitation.

"I'm glad you said something! I hadn't thought of it, but you'd probably like to know some of the stories I have. I bet you haven't heard everything."

"Even if I've heard them, I'd really like to talk about her. I just... It makes me happy."

There was just something really nice about hearing stories of your relative when all anyone ever said about them were good things.

Yes, she supposed that somehow made her proud of her ancestors or maybe inspired her to want to be like them. She wasn't sure. She just knew she'd never get tired of hearing about her gram.

"We can make a time..." Iva May said before her face fell. She leaned a little closer and looked both ways before she said, "John and Anitra didn't say, but John's parents, who live out east, aren't doing well. John and Anitra are concerned they're going to have to take a trip out to help them. I might be working some extra shifts here."

"I could help!" Macy said with her usual forthrightness.

Zoriah noticed Mark's face perked up, but he didn't have the confidence and outgoing personality of his sister, and he didn't say anything.

"Well, how old are you?" Iva May asked.

"I'm seventeen, but I'll be eighteen soon."

"That's perfect. I'm sure we can use you. I'll talk to Anitra and John about it."

Macy sat back with a satisfied smile, confident that she would have a job for the summer.

Zoriah had thought the kids would help her in the store. But maybe it would be good for her to be around other people and get to know the folks in the community.

Zoriah didn't say anything, but she studied Mark.

Iva May had started to turn away, but she stopped and spoke before Mark said anything. "How old are you?"

"Almost fifteen."

Mark's amazed eyes met Zoriah's before Iva May smiled. "I'm sure we can find something for you to do. If you're interested, talk to your aunt, and I'll talk to Anitra and John."

"Yes! I'm interested."

And that was that. Zoriah had been concerned about the kids being bored, but she supposed with both of them working, and with Gage painting the house, maybe they wouldn't have time to be bored and would have a full summer before school started in the fall.

Everything seemed to be working out, and again she thought how great it was that they'd come.

"This might not apply to either of you, but if you're looking to make some money, we have a beach band that did pretty well last year," Iva May said. "Do either of you happen to play an instrument?"

"I played the flute in the marching band at my old school," Macy said right away.

"I played the drums for a little bit," Mark said with his head down, mumbling again.

Zoriah wasn't sure whether she should say something about his mumbling, to correct him so that people could understand when he spoke, or whether she should just let it go. Being a mother was a lot harder than she'd ever thought it was.

She wished her sister were alive so she could tell her that.

"Maybe you two would be interested in joining the beach band?"

"That sounds like a lot of fun!" Macy said. "I'd hoped to keep playing in the school band...does Blueberry Beach High have a band?"

"I think they do. The beach band is something separate, it has a few adults in it and some kids who are younger. But most of the high school kids that are in the beach band also play in the school band. I'll have to introduce you to Sierra and Naomi."

"Naomi Keller?" Macy said.

"Yes. Have you met her?" Iva May asked, sounding surprised, her eyes going to Zoriah's.

"Just today. She works at the candy shop with her sister, Lexi. I spent some time with them there, but then I had to go home and help unpack." Macy's eyes went to Zoriah, but not in an unkind way.

Once again, Zoriah was so thankful that her sister's children were so well behaved. She was also thankful that they seemed to be finding a place in the community on their first day here. She could not ask for more.

She paid for the meal, and they started walking home, assuring Iva May that they would figure out a date to go visit. Before they walked out the door, Iva May said, "Let me give you my phone number. If I have off on the day your inventory arrives, I would love to help you get it set up."

"That would be fantastic," Zoriah said, walking back and giving Iva May her number and telling her she would let her know when it arrived.

They walked home as the sun set. It had gotten cooler, with the brisk April breeze coming in off of Lake Michigan.

"I should have worn a coat," Macy said as she tucked her arms around herself and lowered her head against the wind.

"I should have thought to say something. It does take a little while to warm up this far north, but the wind always makes things colder." She knew it herself, but she'd forgotten. "Sometimes as the sun goes down, the breeze dies down too."

"Hey, look at that," Mark said, pointing to a sign along the sidewalk that said "community yard sale" and had the date for the next Saturday.

"I missed it on our way here, but that sounds like fun," Zoriah said, knowing she probably wouldn't go, since she needed to save every penny in her bank account in order to be able to buy food and other necessities until she was able to open her shop and bring in an income.

She thought of all the stuff she had in storage back in Ohio, but there just wasn't enough time to make a trip.

Hopefully, it wouldn't be long until her shop was turning a profit. Maybe she could have her stuff here for the next yard sale.

"Can we walk on the beach? We haven't even seen it, and we've been here all day," Macy said, and Zoriah smiled.

"Of course. It's gorgeous as the sun goes down."

Maybe, just maybe, Mark and Macy would fall in love with Blueberry Beach and would love it here just as much as she did.

Chapter 5

G age lugged two gallons of paint from the hardware store down the sidewalk. He carried them on one hand, along with his rollers and tray and a few other things he felt he would need in his other hand and stuck in his back pockets.

He whistled. It was a beautiful spring day, the kind of day where a warm breeze was blowing over the lake, and the sky was deep blue, and he felt free and happy and like Blueberry Beach was the best place in the world to live.

He supposed there were places like Blueberry Beach all over the world, but it was his little corner of heaven.

Not that every day was fantastic.

He'd been on a conference call, unusual for a Saturday, and afterward, one of the men that he had been talking to had texted him, letting him in the loop about rumors that the company was going to lay off half of its workforce.

It put a damper in his day, of course. He'd had the job for ten years, and while he didn't exactly love it, he was able to work from home, which made it a good job in his book since he was raising his girls by himself. Blueberry Beach was a wonderful, safe family town. In the summer, there was a lot going on and a lot of tourist money coming in.

Unfortunately, there weren't a whole lot of white-collar jobs, so if he were laid off and wanted to stay, he'd have to find something else online. Which might prove to be impossible.

He wasn't going to worry until it actually happened, although he was going to keep an eye out and be prepared.

There was a fine line there, between worry and being prepared, and he wanted to walk it.

Not panicking, but not burying his head in the sand, either.

He made it to the shop door. Figuring he didn't need to knock, he pulled the door open and walked in juggling everything he carried in his hands.

"Howdy. Beautiful morning," he called out, just so the woman on the stepladder who was wiping the molding at the top of the ceiling would know he was there.

She gasped, turning her head and almost losing her balance on the stepladder, putting her hand on the wall to steady herself.

"Sorry. Didn't mean to scare you."

"It's okay. It's not your fault. And it *is* a good morning."

"Maybe I should get you some bells for over your door."

"I think Grandma had them.... No... She had something...a tone that played 'Jingle Bells,' I believe, when you opened the door. Yes. That's it. 'Jingle Bells.'"

He hadn't thought of that in ages. "That's right. I'm not sure what happened to it," he said, turning around and looking at the door which was bare of any decoration.

"I don't recall seeing it when I helped clean out the store, but maybe she had told someone they could have it, and I might have been too grief stricken to notice."

"That's possible, I suppose. I can ask around if you want me to."

"If she gave it away, I don't want it back. I wouldn't ask someone to return it if she gave it to them. I'll find something else."

"I like 'Jingle Bells.'" He hadn't realized until he stepped in how welcoming it was.

"I did too. July is the busiest time here in Blueberry Beach, and everybody thinks Christmas in July. In fact, if I remember correctly, she often had a Christmas display in the window during July."

He could picture it in his mind immediately. "She did. I remember. The girls always loved to come over and watch it. Usually, it was some kind of moving display. Something she plugged in."

"I haven't gone up to the attic yet." Zoriah spread her hands out, indicating the store. "It's been taking more work than I thought to clean things. Plus I had to go grocery shopping. Before I had children, if I forgot to eat, it wasn't that big of a deal. But now...I can't forget supper."

"Or lunch or breakfast," he added.

"True. Or lunch or breakfast."

He looked around, wondering where the kids were. Zoriah seemed like she was pretty determined to make the store work. He hoped she wasn't going to do more than she could handle. She was taking on a lot of responsibility for one person. He knew firsthand how hard being a single parent was. "Macy's probably old enough to cook. Maybe you should assign her a meal or two."

Zoriah bit her lip and seemed to struggle a little. "I just don't know. I don't know what is asking too much. You know?"

He nodded. He did have an idea. "When I first got divorced, the kids were little, but I felt like I couldn't correct them, I couldn't say no to them, I couldn't not be super dad because then they'd want to go live with their mom. Or they'd hate me more than I already deserved. Or... I don't know what bad thing would happen, but I just had that feeling for a long time."

She nodded, looking relieved that he understood. "Yeah. It's very similar. I guess...I guess I feel like they're always comparing me to their mom. And not that I want to take her place, and not that I think it's a competition. Because I don't." She looked very sincere when she said that, with her eyebrows up and her eyes wide like it was important that he know.

"I believe you," he assured her, because she seemed to need him to.

"I felt like I was kind of saying it like they need to love me, and I want them to, but I don't have any intention of taking their mother's place. I guess maybe I want them to understand that, and maybe that's one of the things that is holding me back."

"I was always afraid someone would come take them from me."

"I guess I'm not afraid of that so much because we don't have any other family members who would be interested..."

"You don't have any other siblings?"

"No."

"You said your parents died in a car accident?"

"That's right." She shifted on the ladder but didn't make a move to come down. "We do have some distant aunts and uncles, but no one beating down the doors to take the kids." She paused. "I wanted them. I was glad no one else did. Or..." She looked around, like she was afraid the children might hear her. "I guess I shouldn't say no one else wanted them. Everyone was just content to let me do it. I just...didn't know it was going to be so hard. And not work-hard, just decision-hard."

"I think you're doing fine from what I've seen. Naomi and Lexi had a good time with Macy, and Macy seems like a well-adjusted kid."

"She is. She's so good. But I do worry sometimes that maybe there are deeper feelings in there that she feels like she can't express. Or I don't know. Maybe I'm just looking for things to worry about." She rolled her eyes and ran her rag over the rung of the ladder. "I'm sorry. You didn't come here to listen to me tell you all the things I worry about."

"No, I understand. Kids like her sometimes seem too perfect, and you wonder if maybe what they think is completely different from what they talk about and say."

She nodded, and he thought they probably agreed on that.

He had no idea and no reassurances. Really, who could know anyone else's heart?

He'd been married to a woman, lived in the same house with her, slept in the same bed, shared a bathroom with her, and didn't know her heart.

He thought maybe it was mostly women who hid so much of themselves, but he'd heard of men doing the same thing to their wives that his wife had done to him, so he couldn't say for sure.

"Give me a minute here to get down off the stool without killing myself, and I'll help you get your stuff set up."

"You don't have to do that. Although if you're in a rush…"

"No. Actually, we have even more time. The distributor that I ordered everything from called earlier and said my order was going to be delayed for a week."

She didn't seem happy about it, probably because she wanted to get the store up and running quickly, but he saw it as a good thing.

"We'll be able to paint the whole store area in that amount of time."

"I didn't want to get too much money sunk into painting until I started having money coming in from the store," she said, biting her lip again. He understood. "I don't want to have you do more than I can pay you for."

"I don't want to be paid. I told you that. I will walk right back out of this store if you insist on it."

He said that with a smile, so she'd know that he meant his words in a friendly way, but he wasn't going to accept payment, especially when he knew that she was struggling just to buy the paint.

She looked down, shaking her head. "I was gone from Blueberry Beach for so long I forgot how it is in small towns like this. I guess you know I'll be looking for a way to pay you back."

"I'll wait until your apparel arrives, and I'll look to see if there's a dress that fits me."

"I'm not sure we can still be friends," she said, a grin tilting her lips up.

He grinned in return, appreciating the fact that she didn't beat around the bush about it or try to pretend that it was okay. "I like a woman who isn't afraid to straight talk me."

"I don't know if that was straight talk or fear."

"Fear?"

"Sure. I'm not entirely sure I'm ready to see your hairy legs yet."

"My legs are offended, madam," he said with a grin.

"I'm sorry, I'm just being honest. Straight talk, remember?"

They laughed together as she showed him where she had drop cloths and produced a stash of masking tape that she'd found in a closet.

"Maybe while you're doing that, I can look around and see where Grandma might have stashed those displays that used to sit in the windows."

"I'd really love it if you could find them, and I'm sure the rest of the town would too. They bring back some great memories for me and my girls as well."

"I told Mark you'd be here at eight o'clock. Maybe I'll run upstairs first and see if he's up and let him know you're down here."

"Sure thing. I brought enough supplies for two people."

"I'm here, Aunt Zoriah," Mark called as he pounded down the rickety stairs. "Hey, Mr. Gage," he said, running into the room with the energy of youth.

Gage grinned. "Good to see you. I was starting to think I was going to have to do this by myself, and I was thinking that maybe I need to go home and think about it a little harder."

Mark laughed. "I've never done anything like this before. I guess you'll have to show me what to do."

He looked a little insecure, and Gage figured he'd much rather have that than overconfidence. He hadn't been quite sure how Mark was going to act.

"There's not much to it, except you want to make sure you don't use too much paint. That's probably the most important thing and the easiest thing to mess up. We don't want to drip everywhere, even though we have drop cloths." He nodded at the cloths that Zoriah had set on one of the clothes racks. "But painting is probably ninety percent preparation."

"Preparation?" Mark asked, tilting his head. "You mean stirring the paint?"

Gage laughed. "No. I mean preparing everything typically takes a lot longer than it actually does to paint. And good prep makes a painting job a lot easier."

By the time Zoriah brought sandwiches down at noon, Mark and he were working in tandem quite well together. Mark proved a quick study, good with his hands, and diligent with what he did, even if he wasn't super talkative, although they had a fairly good conversation going all morning.

He had a feeling Mark would prefer to have earbuds in, but maybe his aunt had told him no.

Before Gage said anything to him about it, he'd have to talk to Zoriah and make sure it was okay.

She seemed like a really nice lady, funny and sweet and totally concerned about making sure she was doing a good job raising her niece and nephew.

He could find a lot in her to admire. He also liked that she loved their small town.

Maybe age gave him better insight, but she was certainly a lot different than the first woman he'd chosen to marry. Not that he was thinking about marriage, but she might be interesting to date.

"Are you two ready to break for lunch?" she asked as she walked in, her smile sincere, her face, while not classically beautiful, fresh and clean and honest.

At this point in his life, he'd go for honest over beautiful any day.

She wasn't hard to look at though, and he grinned at her. "I thought she'd never ask."

She laughed, the sound settling good and right in the chest, the same as it had every time he'd talked to her.

She seemed to laugh a lot, and easily, and he had yet to see her irritated, although he supposed everyone had things they got irritated at.

He certainly did.

"Ham and cheese. Hope that's okay," she said as she handed him a plate with two sandwiches and some chips on it. He grinned at the carrot sticks that lay alongside the chips.

Once upon a time, in his youth, he wouldn't have touched carrot sticks if someone had paid him to.

Age had a way of making a man realize that he wasn't invincible, and he figured he'd probably eat the carrot sticks first.

"Thank you," he said as he took the plate from her, and for just a second, their eyes met, hers smiling and happy, despite the pressure he knew she was under.

Money issues that she couldn't afford to pay for paint, the delayed delivery, and the kids that she wasn't expecting to have to raise herself.

Still, none of that showed on her face, and he liked that she didn't go around with the doom and gloom look all over her. Even though she had every right to.

"Ham and cheese is extra fine if there's plenty of mustard on it." He saw the yellow stuff oozing out and figured she'd put just the right amount on.

"I assumed that's the way you'd want them. There's a ton on there, but I can bring the bottle down if you want me to."

"I see it oozing out the sides. I think I'll be good."

"Thank you," Mark said as he took a plate too.

Gage took a minute to thank the Good Lord for the food He provided and the new friend he had. Even if nothing ever came of the relationship, he and Zoriah were friends.

He assumed Zoriah would go back upstairs and do whatever she was doing, so he was surprised when she carried two more plates down and said, "Macy's coming down with drinks. You don't mind if we join you?"

"I feel bad now. I'd have waited if I knew you were coming down and eating with us," he said, holding a sandwich midair in front of his mouth.

"Don't worry about it. I just was setting things on the table and then realized I might as well come down here, too."

Macy pattered down the stairs behind her and took her plate without saying much.

Gage thought about what they'd said, about Macy having a completely different life inside her head than the one she showed on her face.

For some reason, with the few times he looked at her, he thought that might be true. There was just something...almost sad about her. Even though she smiled and talked at all the right times.

"Where's Naomi and Lexi?" Macy asked, after she bowed her head and said a silent prayer. "I thought we'd see them here today. I thought maybe they'd help us."

"Every once in a while, I let them sleep in on Saturday. Naomi has to be at work at one, so once I'm done eating, I'll probably run over and make sure she's up."

"I can do it," Macy offered quickly.

He lifted his brows at Zoriah, who nodded.

"That's fine. I'll give you the key, because I locked the door when I left." There wasn't crime to speak of in Blueberry Beach, but when his girls were sleeping and he wasn't there, he felt safer with the door locked.

The conversation flowed around them as Mark and Macy asked questions about summertime in Blueberry Beach, and he and Zoriah answered, according to their experiences. He kind of wished his girls had been here, because of the sense of companionable sweetness. Being with Zoriah and her niece and nephew was enjoyable. His girls would have had fun.

He was glad that the opportunity to paint had come up and he was able to spend the time to get to know this family better.

They were a welcome addition to Blueberry Beach.

Chapter 6

Monday morning, Macy and Mark got on the school bus along with Lexi and Naomi and a couple other kids from Main Street, Blueberry Beach.

Zoriah didn't walk out onto the sidewalk with them, and in fact, as they walked out of the front door of the store, she simply waved casually and told them each to have a nice day.

They'd both gone with her when she'd enrolled them in the school on Friday afternoon, so they knew what it looked like and where they were going.

Her casual demeanor was completely fake, though.

She supposed mothers who sent their children off to their first day of kindergarten knew exactly what she was feeling currently as she watched the kids walk out.

This   sick,   scared, I-want-to-go-out-and-bring-them-back-and-not-let-them-go feeling.

They would be fine, and so would she. She'd sent them off to school for weeks after their mother had died and before they'd moved, and she'd been just fine with it. Maybe it was the new location, or maybe it was just she hadn't settled in, even though she felt more comfortable in Blueberry Beach than she had in their old town.

Or maybe it was the fact that their mom had already sent them to school where they were from, but this was completely new and different—a school without their mother ever having seen it.

Whatever it was, Zoriah busied herself with completing the cleaning and moving some things around so Gage could finish his painting this evening after he got off work.

He'd promised to come right over, and she'd promised to cook supper for him.

It wasn't a date.

She enjoyed having him and his girls all day Saturday and Sunday after church. His girls really seemed to get along well with Macy.

The day and a half that Mark had spent working with Gage had basically made the kid idolize him.

Zoriah planned to walk down to the diner after lunch and grab a cappuccino and chat with the ladies there, making sure that everything that her grandmother told her about Gage was accurate.

She felt like he was safe. She even felt a thread of attraction toward him, but smarter women than her had been duped before, and she wasn't going to gamble with the safety of her niece and nephew.

Time flew by as she scrubbed and dusted and wiped, remembering the happy times spent in the shop with her grandmother, playing with the cash register, hiding in the racks of clothing, watching the customers come in.

She had so many cherished memories.

What she hadn't anticipated was the stress on her budget and the stress on herself as she hoped that she would be able to make the store a success and provide Mark and Macy with what they needed.

Her grandmother had always seemed so placid and happy. Never worried or afraid.

Maybe that was just how all adults seemed to children.

She had the two big front windows scrubbed and the areas around them completely clean and planned to look at the attic for the moving displays that her grandmother used to keep in there. It was only April, not near to the Christmas in July when her grandmother used to celebrate, but the Christmas displays were some of her favorites, and if she recalled correctly, her grandmother had five or six different ones.

It would be fun to open the store with the windows decorated for Christmas.

Putting her mop and bucket away, she washed her hands, grabbed her purse, and then looked around for her phone.

Remembering she left it upstairs on the counter as she cleaned off the breakfast dishes, she decided it wouldn't hurt to run to the diner without it.

Iva May greeted her as she walked in, and even though the changes made things seem unfamiliar, walking into the diner was like walking back into her childhood.

"How's the shop coming?" Iva May asked after Zoriah ordered her cappuccino.

"Really well. I'm expecting my delivery to arrive later this week, and I have most of the downstairs clean. Gage has been painting it." Zoriah left her sentence hang there while she fiddled with the napkin holder that sat on the counter.

"It sounds like everything is coming along," Iva May said, a little uncertainly like she knew that Zoriah had more to say.

"It is. But..." She looked around, but no one had come in the deserted diner, and while there were three different patrons sitting at tables, they were along the window, not close enough to hear them. "I was hoping if you could tell me... Macy is really enjoying hanging out with Gage's girls, and Mark follows him around like a puppy dog. I just want to make sure that..." She wasn't sure exactly how to say what she needed to.

But Iva May understood.

"He's a fine man. He's lived here since his wife divorced him. He's been active in the school and community. When Jordan's cancer came back and Anitra couldn't work, Gage helped out. He has a full-time job and wasn't able to do as much as everyone else, but he did a good bit of cleaning—him and his girls—after the diner closed for the night."

Zoriah nodded. It was really all she needed to hear, but Iva May went on.

"Of course he didn't get paid for it, and that's not even really a job that a lot of people knew he did since it was in the evening after everyone left." That almost made it better, in a way, since he obviously wasn't doing it for show. "I really admired that. I already knew he was a good man. That made me admire him more."

Zoriah nodded. "I appreciate you telling me that. I guess we already talked about how I'm not sure if I'm a good mom or not, and I don't want to let my kids go with people that they shouldn't or trust people that I shouldn't."

"I understand. In today's day, you just never know who you can trust some-times. It's a smart lady who watches after her kids." Iva May nodded, her white hair flowing gently up and down with her head.

Iva May moved to make the cappuccino. She called over her shoulder, "I know you just moved in, but maybe you found some things in the apartment that your grandmother stored that you don't want. Have you considered par-ticipating in the community yard sale on Saturday?"

"I wish. But I haven't gone through all Gram's things, since I've been working on getting the shop open. We put almost everything in storage back home."

It had been a lot of work. She'd had her parents' house to clean out, and then her sister's, and then hers. She'd been overwhelmed with stuff. She'd put most of it in storage but donated some to a secondhand store. Which was quite a change from her normal.

She loved going to antique stores and secondhand stores and looking for finds and getting good deals.

"I had three houses to clean out, and I was just overwhelmed with things. We took very little with us. I do have some things in storage back East." She shrugged. "We all have too much stuff, don't we? We get so attached to it. I guess I just didn't have the emotional reserves to deal with figuring out things, especially when I knew Gram's apartment was already fully furnished."

Iva May nodded. "I totally understand."

In a way, Zoriah almost wished she had some things to sell, since her order had been delayed and wasn't coming until later in the week. It would be at least the weekend and maybe next week before she was open.

"I hope I open in time for the yard sale. I think there might be some good business that day. There should at least be a bunch of people running around."

"There sure will, and I bet you're right. People will buy a shirt at the yard sale and come in your shop to find something to wear with it." Iva May turned around, setting the cappuccino on the counter. "I talked to John and Anitra about your niece and nephew."

"Oh?"

Iva May nodded. "Macy is old enough to work here as a waitress, but Mark is too young."

"That might be good. Macy wants to play in the beach band, which I totally support. Music is therapy for the soul." She had grown up in a home that had music.

"You said that like you love it. Do you play something? Adults are welcome in the beach band, too."

"I was actually a music major in college, and I have a BS in music education. I guess that degree is almost as useless as basket weaving." She gave a little laugh, as though it really didn't matter that she'd wasted four years of her life and gotten a degree that she never used, not one day, in her entire life since.

"Couldn't find a job?"

She shook her head. "A lot of schools are doing away with the music and arts programs as well as home ec and shop. I was really thrilled to find out the town of Blueberry Beach had a band."

"It can be a motley crew, since anyone can play, but Mrs. Hershey, the director, donates a lot of time to arranging music at an individualized level, and they practice a lot. But they put an open instrument case out, and people throw money in. As I understand it, they actually made more in the beach band than they would have if they'd been working full time." Iva May lifted her brows at Zoriah's shocked expression.

"Wow. That would be really fantastic for Macy. I haven't even gotten to the point where I'm worried about college tuition, but I should be, I guess. I just feel like it's a success if we get up in the morning and I remember to cook three meals."

Iva May patted her hand. "You'll get used to it."

"I hope so." She sighed and figured that putting on a brave front was point-less. "I wake up every day feeling overwhelmed. I just...don't feel like I'll ever have a handle on everything that I need to."

"Just take it one day at a time, honey. And if that's too much, just look at the next five minutes...the next breath if that's all you can handle. God isn't asking you to do anything more than just live in the moment."

Zoriah smiled, taking her coffee and feeling tension drain out of her at Iva May's words. "That's exactly what I needed to hear. You're right. Just breathe. That's all I'm required to do, and God will help me with that if I forget."

"That's right."

They chatted for a bit more before Zoriah took her coffee and walked back to her grandmother's shop.

Her shop.

So odd to think of it as hers.

Gram would want her to. Gram would want her to face this new chapter of her life with excitement and anticipation and the expectation that everything was going to work out. She wouldn't want her to be biting her lip and worrying over everything. She could almost hear her grandmother saying, "God wouldn't have given you those young 'uns if he didn't think you could handle it. He wouldn't have given you the shop if he didn't think you could handle it, either. So you must be able to handle it."

She didn't need to see her to know what she would say.

With renewed confidence, she walked into her shop, sipping her cappuccino—a treat—and thinking about which Christmas display she wanted to put in the window.

Her favorite one contained a moving merry-go-round with horses and smiling children and couples ice-skating on a pond.

She hoped they were in the attic and that they still worked.

Remembering about her phone, she thought she'd better check her messages and maybe give the Internet tech provider another call. They were supposed to show up this morning to hook up her internet and hadn't.

She did have her computer, but she was on the fence about updating the antique cash register.

Having everything automatically go into a computerized accounting system would shave countless hours off the time that she had to spend doing paperwork and even figuring out what needed to be ordered.

But a system like that would be expensive, and plus, she loved that old cash register.

She thought about the rickety banister as she walked upstairs. Another thing she needed to fix. But with her newfound confidence, she was sure she could figure out how or, if she couldn't figure it out, she could find someone who could.

Reaching the table, she picked up her phone, still really thinking about the banister when she saw the email notification from the distribution company her grandmother had used and that she had ordered her first shipment of supplies for the store from. They'd already delayed it once. Maybe this was the notification that the delivery was on its way.

She skimmed down through the email, then slowed, sinking into a chair, and started reading from the beginning again.

She read it through once more just to be sure before she clicked her phone off and set it down very carefully and very deliberately on the table with the last lines ringing in her head. "We are sorry for any inconvenience this might cause you. Your refund will be processed and applied to your account within thirty business days."

Thirty business days?

She was going to have to make the amount that was in her bank account, along with one last paycheck, last thirty business days, because she couldn't afford to order another shipment and pay for it.

Her heart beat slow and hard and heavy in her chest, and her stomach swished and gurgled and curled, squeezing painfully.

She pushed her chair back a little more until she was far enough away from the table that she could lay her forehead down on the cool metal top. A relic of the sixties or maybe seventies, it was cheap and ugly, she supposed, but it was beautiful to her, because it belonged to her gram. Still, it didn't matter; a table that felt comfortable and familiar wasn't going to help her with this problem.

The temptation to cry was strong, but she could almost hear her gram saying that wouldn't help anything.

She allowed herself a few minutes of pity before she sat up, lifted her chin, and grabbed her phone off the table.

Surely there were places where she could order inventory that wouldn't require payment upfront.

There had to be. And she would find them.

Chapter 7

age hit send on the last email of the day, then powered down his computer.

He didn't hate his day job. It paid the bills but wasn't fulfilling.

His daughters, talking to them, working with them, working to fix their problems and to provide for them, were fulfilling.

Being a part of the Blueberry Beach community, helping at the diner, walking down the street, standing on the shore and looking at the vastness of Lake Michigan and just being awed by it all... That was fulfilling.

Helping his new neighbor get her shop open. That was fulfilling too.

And also exciting. He hadn't expected to look forward to seeing her, hadn't expected to come to enjoy talking with her, to banter and, yeah, even flirt a little with her.

Over the years, he had considered online dating sites, but maybe it was the Lord who had whispered in his ear to just be patient, that if God had someone for him, God was perfectly capable of bringing her around or causing their paths to meet.

He could see Zoriah being the one that God had for him.

But he didn't want to jump the gun. He was too old to make a major mistake like that again.

He and his daughters had paid a heavy price to learn that marrying the wrong woman screwed up your entire life.

Even having a relationship with the wrong woman could mess with your head. Not a good idea.

So it was better to just take things slow and enjoy helping her.

He had a Zoom meeting earlier in the day, so he was wearing a good shirt. He went and changed before he stuck his head in the kitchen where both Lexi and Naomi were sitting at the table, books open in front of them.

"Ready to head over to Zoriah's house for supper?" he asked.

Lexi immediately jumped up with a grin and slammed her book shut.

Naomi was a little slower and didn't look up until Lexi started moving. She pressed the button on her earbud cord.

"What's going on?" she asked.

"It's time to head over to Miss Zoriah's house and eat supper. Remember we talked about it yesterday when you guys stopped in after you got off work at the candy shop."

"Sure," Naomi said, closing up her book and piling it on top of two others. "Did you hear Macy say that she plays flute?" she asked as she put her things in her book bag, not quite as haphazardly as Lexi had.

"I did. I thought you guys were going to help her get set up with the beach band and introduce her to the music director at school."

"Well, about that," Naomi said, leaving the book she'd been working in out and pushing it to the middle of the table.

Gage stopped with his paint rollers in hand. "What?"

"Well, first of all, Macy is like the best flute player I've ever met."

"Macy seems to be really good at everything. She's like the perfect person," Lexi said with her typical penchant for exaggeration. At least, that's what Gage assumed. Maybe Macy really was perfect at everything.

"Everyone has faults. Sometimes, we just don't see them," he said, remembering the feeling he got about Macy keeping her issues to herself. "Sometimes, the people that seem to have everything together are the ones that most need an understanding ear and unconditional love."

Both girls looked at him when he said unconditional love. He supposed he didn't talk about that too often and they were probably trying to figure out exactly what he meant.

"You know, loving someone no matter what. Normally, we think of it like loving someone no matter how mean they are to us. But sometimes, actual perfect people are harder to love. Because..." He lifted a shoulder. "Sometimes, we're jealous. Sometimes, we're upset that they get things that we don't."

He put a hand up as Naomi's brows came down like she was going to deny that she had any feelings like that.

"I'm not accusing you of feeling that way. I'm just telling you you guys looked a little confused when I said unconditional love, and I was trying to explain that it can but doesn't always go in a negative direction. Sometimes, the people we have to work the hardest at loving are the ones that it feels like everyone loves but maybe no one really does."

He wasn't really saying it as well as he could, but his girls seemed to understand, and that's all that mattered.

He realized, though, that he'd gone off on an explanation and almost forgot that Naomi seemed to be hesitating over something.

He checked himself two steps from the door and looked over his shoulder at his girls.

"Naomi? You were going to say something?" he asked.

Naomi shrugged her shoulder. "This feels a little bit like gossip, but I've mentioned about Macy playing the flute, and you'd said about the music director at school, and it just reminded me that the music director...that Mrs. Hershey... Well, I heard today at school that she left her husband and ran off with some dude she'd met online." Naomi looked down, her mouth twisted. She pressed her lips together and kind of mumbled, "I guess that means no more beach band."

Gage stood at the door, blinking, his heart sick and heavy. He hated hearing news like that. Maybe Mrs. Hershey was justified in leaving her husband or felt that way, but a family breaking up was never good news. Still, Naomi was waiting.

"Maybe somebody at the school will take over. Or someone else from Blueberry Beach."

"No, Dad. You don't understand. It has to be someone who knows about music. When we were first playing, we were just doing simple arrangements ourselves, but some of the music that was the most popular was stuff that Mrs. Hershey had taken and written out parts for us so that we all sounded good together. I'm not even sure how she did it. It's just... It was unique to us. And it's not just anybody who can do that."

"I see," Gage said, even though he really didn't, other than whoever directed the beach band had to know more than a little bit about music, which left him out.

He played the trombone in high school, and he'd played with the beach band off and on, but his part had to be pretty simple. He barely read music. He definitely couldn't write it or arrange it.

"I'm sorry to hear that," he said, meaning both that Mrs. Hershey had left her family and also that Blueberry Beach had lost someone who had done so much good for his daughters especially, but tourists and locals alike had really seemed to enjoy the quaint atmosphere the beach band provided. It was almost a throwback to an earlier generation.

Anything that helped people forget about their problems and feel safe and happy and secure was welcome in a town with a lot of vacationers.

A town anywhere, to be honest.

Lexi started talking about something else that happened in school that day, and Gage listened with half an ear as he opened the door and allowed his girls to walk out ahead of him.

Zoriah had been excited about the beach band and about Macy getting involved in the community. He hated that they would be disappointed. But maybe she'd find a job at one of the shops or something else could come up. He hoped.

Macy seemed like the kind of girl that could get herself involved in anything, but sometimes that could prove to be a liability if the things she got involved with weren't the right ones.

He had his own girls to worry about though, and he never figured there was any point borrowing trouble, so he didn't.

Mark actually came running out of the shop and jogged across the street to meet them as they walked out from between the buildings on the other side of the street.

"You guys need to hurry. I'm starving!" Mark greeted them.

"You're always hungry," Naomi said dismissively, like she'd grown up with a little brother and knew it somehow.

He supposed Mark was only a few years younger than Naomi, but in high school, a couple of years felt like decades.

"Relax. It won't be long now," Gage said as Mark turned around and started walking beside him as the girls walked on ahead.

"Do you need me to carry something?" Mark asked, eyeing the paint roller in his hand and the extender he'd brought along.

If he had enough time, he was going to paint the ceilings too. But he wanted to get the walls finished first.

"You sure can," he said, handing the paint roller over.

"You could clean this up at our place," Mark said. "Then you wouldn't have to carry it over to your house."

"I didn't want to make a mess in your aunt's sink. I already have some paint splashes on mine that I need to scrape off. A few more aren't going to make that much of a difference."

"Hmm," Mark said, and Gage had an idea.

"Maybe you'd like to come over this evening with me after I'm done, and I'll show you how I clean them."

"I'd love that!" Mark said, confirming the hunch that Gage had had.

"You think it would be hard, and it's really not, but you do need to make sure you get them clean, otherwise they'll be hard and crusty when you go to use them, and they'll put the paint on unevenly."

"I bet I can do it. You just run water over it?"

"Sure. That's pretty much it. You just have to be diligent to get it all."

They'd reached the door, which Naomi was holding open, but Gage stopped before he went through.

"Looks like your Aunt Zoriah was busy today," he said, looking at the Christmas display that was working in the window. It was one of his favorites, with the horses and merry-go-round and skaters. "Looks like all the pieces are working. I think she was concerned that they wouldn't be."

"Aunt Zoriah was so excited about it that she was standing right inside the door waiting for us to get off the school bus so she could tell us about it and show us," Mark said, stopping beside Gage as they stared at the display in the window.

"This is gonna make a lot of people in Blueberry Beach pretty happy. I'm sure I'm not the only one that's missed this for the last two years since your great-grandmother passed away."

"I love that one! It's my favorite," Lexi said, coming back out the door and staring through the glass. "Although I really like the one with the Santa sleigh that hangs down from the ceiling and it looks like it's flying. Rudolph's nose even glows red in that one."

Gage nodded at his daughter. "I like that one too. There's just something magical about seeing it suspended in the air."

"That's the way I feel about the angels that hang down. There's only a couple of moving parts on that one, like the donkey's head and a wise man kneeling or something, but I just love seeing those angels even though I don't think they were really holding hymn books when they were singing in the sky."

Gage laughed. "I think you're probably right. I'm guessing angels probably don't need hymn books. And they probably weren't singing hymns, but hey, maybe they were."

They laughed together as they moved on into the store.

Chapter 8

G age set the supplies down in the shop area, and he followed the girls and Mark up to the apartment, watching the banister wiggle and wondering if he would be able to fix it.

He'd done a few handyman things around his apartment, and if he'd ever wanted an actual house rather than an apartment, it would have been so that he would have a shop or garage in which to work. In high school, he'd made different wood carvings and tried his hand at some furniture. It was a hobby he enjoyed, although nothing that would ever support him, and so the idea of buying a house with a garage wasn't anything that he'd ever pursued, because it would require moving off Main Street in Blueberry Beach.

He loved living here, loved raising his girls here, and didn't want to relocate.

One major move—after his divorce—was enough.

They walked in the house kitchen, and Zoriah was all smiles. She seemed happy and bubbly to the point where he actually said, "You must've gotten some good news today."

A shadow passed over her face. He was a terrible judge of emotions, but he would almost say it was the opposite.

But her lips smiled as she shook her head. "Nope. It's just a beautiful day, and we're all healthy, and we're all together. I guess that's a good enough reason to be happy, isn't it?" she asked and then turned back to the counter where she was mashing the potatoes with a hand mixer.

"Can I help with something?"

"You can carry the skillet to the table," she said immediately.

"Sure. I don't know what it is, but it smells delicious."

"It's a thing my grandma used to make, and it's pretty simple, using ground round, but it tastes really good and is a kid favorite."

He shared a smile with her and realized that maybe she wasn't sure what his girls would like.

Macy was telling everyone where they could sit, and Mark had been given the job of filling everyone's glass up with water.

Maybe there was not a whole lot of affection between Mark and the girls, but they seemed to get along okay. He tucked that back in the corner of his mind.

He liked to think that he wouldn't even consider having a relationship with someone who had children who didn't get along with his.

Maybe he was thinking about it the wrong way, but he felt like his kids should come first, since they had gotten such a short stick with the divorce.

He'd been willing to work things out, but his wife hadn't been interested.

And now that he had time to consider Mrs. Hershey, it grieved him even more, because if he was correct, she had kids in school.

It was like his wife all over again, only his wife had insisted she was moving up in the world.

Hopefully, Mrs. Hershey hadn't done that as well.

It happened so long ago he couldn't believe he was dredging memories. But maybe it was because of hearing about Mrs. Hershey combined with the idea tickling in the back of his head that Zoriah would be an easy woman to fall in love with.

If she didn't have so much on her plate already.

He just needed to be patient. He'd waited this long—more than a decade since his divorce—he could wait a little longer.

Although he wasn't getting any younger.

They settled at the table, said grace, and began passing food, the kids talking about the bus ride, which they shared, and then discussing what might happen with the beach band.

Mark was less interested in the band, since drums were the only instrument he played, and they had assumed that they wouldn't have those in the band.

"Maybe the only reason they didn't have drums was because they didn't have anyone to play them," Zoriah said, answering a comment that Macy had made, but that went along with what he'd been thinking.

"Sure. I'm sure that's it," Naomi said. "Maybe whoever takes over Mrs. Hershey's spot will write you in. We already have all the music we've learned, so all we need is someone to write a part for you."

"I'll need a part, too," Macy said. "Or do you think I won't be able to join now?" she asked, biting her lip.

"Oh! Of course you will. You'll just copy the flute part. It's already been written. And you'll play the same thing as the other flutist," Naomi explained, and Macy's face once again settled down into a smile.

"Do they have any idea who they're going to get to replace Mrs. Hershey?" Zoriah asked as she passed the mashed potatoes to Mark.

Gage bit his tongue in order not to say something as Mark put three scoops of mashed potatoes on his plate.

He figured it would make the boy self-conscious for him to tease him about how much he was eating, but it was still tempting. It was also tempting to put three scoops on his own plate, but he assured himself he could come back for seconds.

"Do you know how long it's been since I've had homemade mashed potatoes?" he asked.

Zoriah smiled, like his question had pleased her. She picked up the broccoli and scooped some onto her plate. "I don't make them that often. It's not easy to make mashed potatoes for one person." Her eyes went around the table. "Or even three people."

"So that's my excuse. It's hard to make homemade mashed potatoes for just three people. Remember that, girls."

"I've never even seen mashed potatoes being made," Lexi said, her face scrunched up like she was remembering how she'd seen Zoriah making them when she walked in and couldn't quite believe how it was done.

"I never even thought of having you girls over to help me today. Next time if you're interested, we'll have mashed potatoes and I'll teach you exactly how it's done," Zoriah said, grinning at them with a little twinkle in her eyes.

Lexi especially perked up, and Gage wondered if maybe he should have put more effort into finding a mother for her and Naomi.

It wasn't all about him and his relationships, although that's what it took to keep them together.

He supposed he could assure Zoriah that she wasn't the only one that second-guessed herself. Just because she was new at parenting didn't mean that she was the only one who doubted whether or not she was doing the right thing.

They finished eating, talking a little more about the music and discussing the decorations in the window. They all helped clean up, then his girls and Macy walked back across the street to finish their homework together. Mark went down with him while Zoriah washed the dishes and put the food away, promising to come down later.

By the time eight o'clock rolled around, he was completely finished with all of the walls and had gotten everything taped up to start on the ceiling the next evening.

Zoriah had come down and watched for the last ten minutes as they finished up the last of the paint and put everything away.

"Would you like some ice cream?" he asked as he gathered the last of his things up to take over.

"I think I'll pass tonight, but thank you."

"If you don't mind, I told Mark he could come over, and I'd show him how I clean everything up. "

"I don't mind at all," Zoriah said, and he hesitated, because she'd already shut down his idea of ice cream.

But then he figured he didn't really have anything to lose. "You provided supper, so if you don't mind, I'd like to treat the kids at least to ice cream. Is that okay?"

She bit her lip, like she didn't want to accept anything from him. He wasn't sure exactly what the trouble was, but he had suspected it was something along those lines. Which is why he'd reminded her that she'd provided supper.

"I guess it's okay," she said. "I just... I just feel bad that you're buying it for them."

"I offered. I'm honored that you've accepted," he said, and he and Mark started walking toward the door.

Before he reached it, he decided to be really bold, and he stopped and turned around.

"Maybe instead of ice cream, you'd like to walk along the beach? It's a warm evening with a pretty moon." He'd been able to see it through her big picture windows in front.

He thought she was going to turn him down for that too, and she started shaking her head, but he met her eyes, figuring it was always harder to tell someone no when they were looking at you, and she gave him a self-conscious smile.

"I'd enjoy that. We've been down to the beach once since we moved in, but I haven't been there at night, and I know it's pretty."

"That sounds great. Give me a few minutes to go over and get these things taken care of. Maybe the kids will grab an ice cream and join us."

She nodded, like it was less intimidating if the kids were there, as he figured.

He had to remember not to hurry through cleaning his equipment but to take his time and show Mark exactly how it should be done. It had been a long time since he walked on the beach with someone, more than a decade, and he was looking forward to it.

He also had a couple of questions he wanted to ask Zoriah without the children around. Questions Zoriah might not think were any of his business, but he figured since they were neighbors, he might be able to get away with them.

Chapter 9

Zoriah regretted agreeing to go for a walk.

It had been hard enough to get through supper, even with the kids around, and not say anything about her worries and about the email that she'd gotten.

She wasn't sure she would be able to keep from mentioning it tonight. She'd already said more to Gage than she should have about her private matters, but the man was just so easy to talk to. And he'd listened with genuine interest while she spoke. She hadn't even realized how much she'd unburdened on him until after he'd left. She'd vowed not to do it again.

But maybe it didn't matter. Maybe she was supposed to be able to talk to him. Maybe that was the whole point of God giving her a neighbor who was coming around, not just painting, but coming with his girls and eating with them, giving her words of wisdom she'd needed, and now walking on the beach with her as well.

Regardless, she sat in her big empty shop, the shop that was going to stay empty for weeks, until she saw Gage come out from between the buildings with Mark and the girls.

He pulled out some bills from his wallet, handed the money to them, and started across the street as they headed up to the ice-cream shop.

Zoriah walked out the door, wondering if maybe she should have brought her keys down and locked it but figuring it would be okay. Blueberry Beach was such a safe town.

She stood in front of her door as Gage walked out.

"Ready?" he asked.

"I am."

He had been right; the evening was warm for April, and the moon bright. It was a beautiful night for a walk. The scent of spring hung in the air, and Lake Michigan glowed like a big black diamond in the distance.

"The kids said they were going to sit at the tables and eat. Apparently, Sierra is working tonight, and they wanted to chat with her. Have you met her?"

Zoriah scrunched her brows. "I believe she's Lindy and her husband's daughter?"

"Right. Adam is his name. She's in between Naomi and Lexi in age, and they're pretty good friends. I'm sure Macy will fit right in with their group."

"I'm so happy. I had been concerned about them having good friendships. That's important."

"I know. I'm glad they're all getting along too, although Mark does seem like the odd man out."

"You've taken him under your wing, and I really appreciate that. I do believe he's made some friends at school, and one of them lives just up the street, but he's learning a lot from you, and it's really nice that he has such a great example." Zoriah put her head down and shoved her hands in her pockets, figuring she should just go ahead and be honest before the word got out from someone else. "I did ask about you at the diner today. I hope that was okay."

"I like it. What did you ask, whether or not I was married?"

She laughed, assuming he was just being funny to put her at ease.

"I already knew that, of course." They turned toward the beach and started walking down the sidewalk toward the break in the dunes. "I asked Iva May if I was right to trust you, because I don't want to make a mistake with the kids. Iva May assured me that you were better than the Pope pretty much."

"Well, I don't have any personal knowledge of the Pope, but I'll take that as a compliment."

"I guess I meant it that way, although you're right. I don't know the Pope either. I suppose it could have been an insult."

"I hope not."

"The intention was a compliment," Zoriah said deliberately. "How about that?" It was a huge relief that he wasn't upset, and he almost acted like it was an okay thing for her to be cautious.

"Perfect." He paused a little and looked to the side. She could be wrong, but she thought he was biting his lip and had something he wanted to say.

She walked in silence, waiting.

"I suppose I could go to Iva May." He gave a little emphasis there, like he was teasing her for going to Iva May instead of asking him. "But I'll just go ahead and ask you, since this question concerns you."

"Maybe I would rather you go to Iva May."

"I'm not sure she has the answer."

"Now you're scaring me."

"Well, that's good. You should be afraid. Very afraid." He had such a goofy inflection in his voice that she couldn't help but laugh and be totally unafraid. She had been convinced, in the week they'd been here, that he had only her best interest at heart.

She wasn't sure how much deeper his interest went, but the more time she spent with him, the more she hoped that it went deeper than just surface friends.

She tried not to hold her breath as she waited for him to speak.

"Feels like there was something bothering you tonight. I was wondering what was," he finally said in a soft, serious voice and a little low, like he knew he was way overstepping but was determined to ask anyway.

His words, perceptive as they were, made her bite the inside of her cheeks to try to keep the back of her throat from closing and her eyes from filling with tears.

Funny how different things could make a person cry. Losing their parents. Watching their sister fade away. Thinking about their orphaned niece and nephew.

And yet, having someone care. Having someone notice that she was struggling, that she had something weighing heavy on her heart, that...she had a burden that was pulling her down.

Funny how that could make a person want to cry the same way an overwhelming sadness could.

"Zoriah?" he prompted, and Zoriah realized she'd been quiet for too long, but she still couldn't find the words.

"I'm sorry. I didn't mean to pry." Then right away, he grunted. "Never mind that. I did mean to pry. I just thought... I guess we've only known each other a week, but I thought that maybe we're good enough friends and neighbors that I could take advantage of that and push a little." There was a pause as they took two more steps before he said, "There is something wrong, isn't there?"

Their feet had hit the sand, and they walked out through it. Zoriah had worn flip-flops, and while Gage hadn't changed his clothes, he'd taken his sneakers off and put sandals on.

Neither of them removed their footwear as they went closer toward the water's edge where the sand hardened.

"You're right. I'm sorry. I was trying to be happy and not make everyone feel bad, and I guess I wasn't successful."

"The opposite. You were a little more happy and bubbly than what you'd normally been, which is what clued me in on maybe there was something wrong. Then, I guess I did see a few shadows cross your face, and it just made me wonder what was going on."

Their feet hit the harder sand and pebbles along the shore where it was easier to walk, and when Gage turned to the left, she turned with him.

"You don't have to tell me unless you want to, of course," he said.

"No. I guess I was just thinking about what to say."

She sighed, blowing it out and touching her tongue to her lips. She didn't want to make herself sound pathetic, but she supposed she should just lay the truth out, without trying to sugarcoat it.

"I used almost all the money that I had to order inventory for the store. I had to pay for it before they would ship it, and I just got an email today from the place I ordered from saying that they were canceling my order, and they would refund my money."

He let her words digest, and she appreciated that he seemed to really be thinking about them.

"Okay. So maybe you'll have a delay of a week?"

Oh, she'd left the most important part out. "It is going to take a month to refund it back into my account. Maybe they'll do it sooner..." She kind of trailed off, her disbelief plain in her tone.

"Oh."

"Which probably shouldn't be terrible, but my sister had a lot of medical bills. She left everything to me, but it took everything she had, plus everything I did, to pay off her bills. I wasn't too worried about it at the time, because I had a good job, but then when we decided to move, I used everything I had left from the sale of my home to purchase that shipment."

"I see. And you were banking on making money from that to pay your bills and buy more."

"Exactly. And my bills aren't that high. My car is paid for, and I don't have a house payment of course but..."

"You have to live on something. Eat. Electricity."

"Sure. And then there are all the unexpected things that come up. We got a tax bill in the mail the day after we moved. And I have some fees involved in purchasing licenses and the things I needed in order to start the business. I can use the old cash register, but having a new system would make things so much easier..." She was rambling now, and she deliberately shut her mouth, gathered her words, and summed it up by saying, "There are just a lot of things. And it's scary to me to see my checkbook down below three figures and have absolutely no idea what I'm going to do."

"Are you getting any more paychecks from your last job?" Then he put a hand up, in a stop position. "Forget that. That was too nosy."

"No," she said with a little laugh. "I've just basically told you my entire financial history. You're entitled to a few questions that maybe on a different night or in a different conversation might be considered nosy. They'll deposit my last check in my account on Thursday."

"So you'll be able to buy groceries at least."

"Yes. I can feed the kids." She laughed again, more because of her tension than because anything was funny. "I don't think we're quite completely desperate, but yeah. I do have a few bills sitting on my desk. Nothing that can't wait, although once you get behind, it's probably really hard to catch up again."

"I'm sure. You end up having to double pay everything. Let's try not to let that happen."

She loved how he was saying "let's," but she had to remind him, "This isn't your problem. I didn't mean to drag you into it. I just...needed to talk to someone and get it off my chest."

"You didn't drag me in. I asked, remember?"

"I think you already used that line on me once today. It loses its effectiveness after the first time."

He smiled at her maybe pathetic attempt at humor. "Maybe for you. It's just as effective for me the second and third and fourth time if necessary."

"I guess we'll have to agree to disagree on that one."

"I guess so." They went a little further in silence, their feet making muted swishing sounds on the sand and the waves of the majestic lake beside them splashing in a natural, relaxing rhythm.

Gage said, "I kind of have a few ideas in my head. I know that this is something that you probably don't want the entire town talking about, but I guess you figured out by now that things haven't changed too much from when you grew up here. We all kinda stick together and take care of each other. So if you don't mind, I'd like to run this by a couple of people and see what they say."

"You have ideas?" She wanted to know what they were. She felt stuck and hopeless. Could there be a way she wasn't thinking of?

"How stuck are you on having a clothing store?"

"Well...only because my grandmother did."

"As I recall, she didn't usually have the store completely full, right? She typically had some displays, kind of like the Christmas ones in the window now. Just fun stuff to take up floor space and make it not look so empty?"

"I suppose that's true. I had been thinking I would get a few more things down and set them up, but I wanted to see how the apparel that I had ordered looked first." She couldn't figure out what he was driving at and figured she had a right to know. So she pressed a little further. "Why? Does this have something to do with your idea?"

"Yeah. I guess it won't hurt to tell you, although I was thinking I didn't really want to get your hopes up if the townspeople aren't interested or won't go along with it. I don't want you to feel hurt or upset."

"I wouldn't. No one owes me anything. I'm not expecting anyone to get me out of this mess. I wouldn't have even told you if you hadn't asked." She grunted though and kicked at the sand with her foot. "Although I can't guarantee that I wouldn't have told some people. It feels like a heavier weight than I can handle right now. I was hoping I could crawl out of the hole that I was in before I land in another one that's even deeper."

"I guess I know the feeling. I felt like that after my divorce. It's hard enough to take care of the kids, and then when Lexi had some complications from the chickenpox, and Naomi had trouble learning to read at school, and then my employer told me they were downsizing and closing the office building I was working in, I felt like everything was crashing down around me, but it turned out okay because while they closed my office building, they kept me on if I agreed to work from home, which was the biggest blessing ever, because I was able to move here." He let her digest that and then added, "It felt like the end of the world, but everything turned out for good, even better than what it had been."

He stumbled a little, and Zoriah narrowed her eyes at him.

"There's something you're not saying in that story, isn't there?"

His grin was guilty. She knew it.

She pointed her finger at him. "Tell."

Chapter 10

"After everything you told me, I guess you deserve to know." Gage's smile faded a little as he looked away from Zoriah and back down the beach. "It's not nearly as bad as what you're going through, but this week, I heard some rumors from a couple of the people I work with that my employer might be laying half the workforce off. That doesn't necessarily mean that I'm losing my job, but I could. And while I feel pretty confident that I can find something, and I do have a good bit of money saved away, I was hoping to be able to help the girls with their college tuition, and I wasn't expecting to have to use it to float myself while I went job hunting. Not a big deal," he said, shrugging his shoulders, but Zoriah wasn't fooled.

"Any time your job's in jeopardy, it's scary. You could lose your health insurance."

"Yeah. You're right. So I guess it is a big deal, but I'm not worried about it. The person I talked to typically does hear a lot of accurate rumors, but that's all they are right now, rumors."

"I see. Obviously, I hope things work out for you. It would be terrible for our end of the street if both of us are out of work. Which..." She tilted her head and looked at him. "What was your idea?"

He laughed. "I couldn't even distract you with my problems, could I?"

"Nope. I'm like a hound on the scent," she said, trying for a little bit of goofy, because the night had been so serious.

"Do you want to turn around and start walking back?" he asked.

"Are you changing the subject again?" she asked, even as she stopped and waited for him to turn with her.

"Maybe."

They laughed together, and then he said, "Seriously, I don't want to get your hopes up, but I was thinking...you've heard of the community yard sale that's supposed to be happening on Saturday?"

"Of course. It's a big deal. Someone said you even took up a collection and advertised in some bigger papers, trying to draw nonlocals in. I hope it works out for you all."

She couldn't figure out what that had to do with her. Maybe he was going to suggest she make ham and cheese sandwiches to sell? She probably could. Although she didn't really want to take business away from the diner. Maybe she could stand on the sidewalk and grill hot dogs or buy sodas and sell them.

She probably wouldn't make a killing, but maybe she'd make enough to tide them over for the month.

She wasn't prepared for his idea.

"I was thinking we should cancel it, and everyone can give their things to you, and maybe find a few more things to donate, and you could open up a used clothing shop or a secondhand store in general and carry more than just clothes. Books, kitchenware, antiques even? I mean, tourists are going to be here. They're going to find things here that they might not be able to find at home. It might be interesting to them."

"Oh my goodness, no!" Zoriah exclaimed. "I couldn't ask everyone to do that! I just... Some people are probably counting on the money they'll make at the yard sale." She shook her head, looking at the gray sand as it passed underfoot in the soft moonlight.

"We don't have to have them cancel the yard sale. We could just suggest that donating to you is something they could do." Gage sounded like he wasn't the slightest bit put off by her protest. "Is that really the reason you're against it?"

Her head snapped up, and she turned to look at him, her brows drawn in, her mind tumbling. What was he trying to ask? What other reason could she have?

"I don't understand? Of course that's the reason. I couldn't ask people to make such a big sacrifice just to keep me in business or to get me in business. Especially since I haven't seen any of them for years and we're not that close. It's not like they're helping a relative."

"Well...I was thinking that you might not want to have a used clothing store. Or a secondhand store. Maybe you had your heart set on apparel like your grandmother."

"No," she said with a little bit of a laugh. "I want to open my grandma's store, true. And I do have memories of clothes, but there are so many other things that are associated with the store. Not just what she sold, but the spirit that was in it."

His body seemed to relax, like he knew what she was talking about. "That's what we missed more than anything when her store closed and she passed away. It wasn't the fact that there was no place to buy scarves or skirts. It was that Grandma Heater wasn't there anymore with her displays in the windows and the chocolate and cinnamon scent that always surrounded you when you went into her store, or her smile, and her big hugs and just the personality that was there."

"Me opening the store might not replace that." She hadn't even thought about stepping into her gram's shoes in that way. She'd just been thinking about getting the store open, paying bills, and keeping her niece and nephew fed with a roof over their heads.

The idea that there were shoes to fill, a space like that, a personality to replicate, it made her doubt herself, although not for the first time, but in that way for the first time.

Her steps slowed, and she put her arms around her waist. "Maybe I can't do it. I'm not anything like my grandma. She was so... She just knew what people needed before they even knew sometimes, and she knew how to give them whatever it was that would make them happy. I don't have that," she said softly, wishing she were alone with her insecurities. They seemed too tender and personal to share. Although up until that point, she'd been enjoying the company of the steady man beside her.

Calm and sweet, the perfect mixture of strength and compassion, he felt like someone she could depend on. It was a good feeling and one she hadn't been afraid to embrace. But his words had made her worry that she wasn't going to be enough.

"I don't think you need to be your grandma," he said slowly. "You'll just be you, and it will be perfect. Whatever life you bring to the store, maybe a combination of the old, with the displays in the same location and you look similar to your grandma in some ways. You have her smile." He smiled over at her, and her lips turned up in return. "Plus, we know there will be things you do that she didn't. I was never around when you and your sister were growing up, but Macy and Mark will be there. They'll be different but still teenagers in the store."

He sighed and looked out on Lake Michigan, deep and dark.

"Communities are always growing and changing. When we're little, we feel like they'd been the same way forever, because we didn't know what they were like before we were born, at least we didn't experience it. You'll just be part of the change, and it will be a positive change. I'm sure of it."

His words reassured her, and her doubts, if they didn't quite slip completely away, at least got smaller.

"I'll take your word for it, and I'll work to be a positive change," she finally said. "But that doesn't change the fact that whether I have a secondhand store or whether I have a new apparel store, I can't ask Blueberry Beach to cancel their community yard sale in order to donate things so my store can open. I just can't."

"I understand," Gage said softly, and while she was surprised at his easy capitulation, she appreciated it and felt like he really did understand.

They walked a little more in silence, almost to the spot where the path went through the dunes and into the beach parking lot that was at the end of Main Street, Blueberry Beach.

Full darkness had fallen, although with the moon and the reflection on the water, she could still see bodies as her eyes skimmed over the beach, noting that it seemed like there were more people than what she would expect for an April evening.

Her eyes hooked on one person, and she squinted. The body looked familiar, standing in a crowd of rougher-looking people.

Surely it wasn't Macy. She was supposed to be with Gage's girls, but the people that familiar-looking person was standing with weren't any kids Zoriah knew. They didn't look like teenagers at all.

She almost said something to Gage, asking him about it, but the group broke up. The people she didn't recognize walked out to the beach and headed in the opposite direction from Gage and Zoriah, while the one that looked like Macy walked back toward the parking area.

She realized she'd picked up the pace and was now walking a couple yards ahead of Gage.

"Are you cold?" he asked, catching back up to her as she slowed down.

"No," she said, again tempted to ask if he thought it was Macy, but the person had disappeared beyond the dunes, and she couldn't see them anymore anyway. "I'm sorry, I guess I just kinda got in my head and didn't realize I'd started walking faster."

"If you're in a rush, we can hurry, but I was kind of enjoying both the scenery and the company."

"Me too," she said, more shyly than she wanted to.

What was she doing? She should be enjoying a romantic walk on the beach with the good, solid man beside her. She hadn't had too many of those—romantic walks—in her life. But instead of enjoying it, she was looking at people and seeing things that weren't there.

What would Macy be doing with people like that? Especially when she was supposed to be hanging out with Naomi and Lexi?

"Maybe we can do it again?"

It only took a half a step for her to respond. "I would like that."

Maybe her voice sounded a little breathless, maybe she sounded a little eager, and maybe she sounded a little infatuated as well. Rightfully so, because she was all of those things.

"I enjoyed your homecooked supper, but I guess if we do this again, I should provide it."

"I enjoy cooking. And I'd like for Macy to learn if she's interested. And Naomi and Lexi seemed interested as well. It would be fun to have them over to cook at times."

"We'll have to see that that happens."

They'd reached the opening to the dunes, and they walked through on the narrow trail before stepping onto the sidewalk. And, as though they talked about it, they moseyed on down to the ice-cream shop.

Looking in the window, they could see the place was deserted aside from a blonde behind the counter.

"It's a school night, and I bet the girls went back to finish their homework. Do you want to come up and see?"

His question hung there, and Zoriah wasn't sure what to say.

She wanted to spend more time with Gage, and she was curious as to what his apartment looked like, and she definitely wanted to go with him, but seeing that person who looked similar to Macy had made her a little anxious, and she was eager to get back to her apartment.

Plus, she didn't want to take advantage of Gage, especially if he was only being nice.

"Thank you for inviting me, but I think I better get home. Like you said, it's a school night, and if Macy and Mark aren't at your place, then they're probably home and I should be as well."

"I'll walk you across the street," he said, turning toward her side.

She laughed. "You don't have to do that. Just stay here, and you can watch me if you really have to," she said, feeling...almost cherished by the idea that he wanted to make sure that she was okay.

"Humor me. I want to walk you."

She didn't want to argue, so she just nodded her head, and they walked across the street.

"There. Nothing happened to me. Thank you." She smiled up into his eyes, warmed by the look he was giving her as he looked down at her. It was affection and humor and maybe something even deeper. She wasn't sure, but she couldn't recall too many people looking at her like that, even the long-term relationships that she had. And she liked it.

"Thank you for a wonderful evening," she said softly.

"Thank you. Thank you for delicious food, and great company, and a few laughs, and some wonderful conversation."

She lifted her brows. "I'm not sure I can claim all of that, but it's nice of you to say so."

"You can. Maybe I'll see you tomorrow evening when I go over to paint."

"I'm sure you will. I'll make sandwiches for supper."

"Sounds good. Good night."

He waited until she'd walked into her store and locked it behind her before he strolled back across the street. She watched him go, a smile on her face, even as her brain said she was too old to look at a man with dreamy stars in her eyes. Then she picked up her phone, texting Macy and Mark, making sure they were in before she put the chain lock on the door and walked up the stairs.

Chapter 11

The next morning, Gage started work a little early, putting out all the fires that had started overnight and finishing up a project that was due at the end of the week.

He made a couple phone calls, updated a shared spreadsheet, and then took his phone and walked out of his apartment.

One of the nice things about working from home was that he didn't have to be at his house all the time, as long as his work got done. He didn't even have to work nine to five, as long as he took care of everything he needed to.

Typically, he put in at least a full eight hours, because that was right, and sometimes, he put in more.

Although nothing said they had to be eight full hours sitting in front of his computer at his desk in his house.

Today was one of those days he was taking advantage of that, because he wanted to talk to Iva May and Beverly.

Zoriah had been completely against the idea of canceling the yard sale and donating the things people were going to sell to her store. She had a point that some people might be counting on that income. So maybe his proposal had kind of changed from wanting to cancel the yard sale to wanting to offer people the chance to donate their things to her store, instead.

He didn't want people to feel like they had to, but he didn't think that would be a problem.

He thought people would be eager to help someone open a store in Grandma Heater's spot.

"Good morning, Gage. You want your usual?" Iva May greeted him as the bells jingled above his head when he walked into the Blueberry Beach diner.

"Please." He looked around, noting that the breakfast rush had cleared out and the lunch rush hadn't started yet. "Would you have a few minutes to chat with me?" he asked as Iva May made his coffee.

"I sure would. I'd love to." Iva May's eyes twinkled, and she truly did look happy for the opportunity to sit and chat with him.

It took her a few minutes to mix up his usual, and then she came around the counter and they walked together to a table right by the counter in case someone walked in.

"Have you ever considered slowing down? Every time I come in, you're here?"

"I love it. I love seeing people every day and talking to them. It keeps me young, I think."

Iva May with her rosy cheeks and snow-white hair and twinkling eyes reminded him of Mrs. Claus, but there was a sadness lurking in her eyes, there always was, but some days, it seemed more prominent. This was one of those.

He didn't figure he would be able to help her with anything—he was the one always going to her for advice—so he didn't ask. That wasn't what he had come to talk about, anyway.

"I know everyone here was excited when Zoriah came and we all found out that she was going to open Grandma Heater's store." That seemed like a good opening line.

"We sure are. There's just been something missing since it closed."

"Do you feel like it has to be an apparel store?" he asked, figuring that the answer to that question was important for the other questions that he wanted to ask.

Iva May tilted her head a little, and her eyebrows popped up but only for a few seconds, before she started shaking her head and lifted her shoulder. "Of course not. It's just the idea of having the store there. It's more Grandma Heater's spirit and the feeling that you get from knowing that she was down there...her life and her laughter and just going by her store and seeing how beautifully she had it decorated and just having her around with us." Her brows drew down, and she seemed to study him. "Why?"

"Because I suggested to Zoriah that she should open a secondhand store instead. The upfront costs are less, and she could probably even put a collection bin outside her building and get a lot of interesting things from tourists. Maybe vacation clothes that they'd bought just for vacation, ones that don't fit, or towels and sandals and who knows what all they would get. I think it would be interesting and fun for her and for vacationers."

Iva May pursed her lips while she tapped her finger on the table. "I think that's a great idea. But doesn't she want to sell apparel?"

"I think there are some financial issues." She hadn't sworn him to secrecy, but if he didn't need to talk about the details, he wasn't going to.

"She would still have to put money out to buy used. The yard sale would be a great place for her to start shopping. This Saturday. How soon was she thinking of opening?"

"Well...I had some things I was going to put in the yard sale, but I thought I would donate them to her instead, to help her get her store started."

"That's a great idea! That would be super helpful for her. Especially if there are financial issues. I suppose, with her sister being sick so long, and all the things that entails, she probably doesn't have a lot of extra money."

"I don't think I'm at liberty to say exactly. But I do think that a secondhand store would make her just as much profit and also cost her less to start. Two good things."

"I see. How about I ask around and see if anyone else is interested? I had several boxes that I was going to set up, but if Zoriah can use them, I'll give them to her. I didn't need the money, I just wanted to get rid of the junk."

"Talking about getting rid of junk?" Beverly said as she walked in the door and strode to their table.

Gage had heard the door open, but he hadn't turned around to see who walked in.

"Hi, Miss Beverly." He smiled, standing and putting a hand out. "You can sit down if you'd like."

"I just dropped in to see Iva May and say hi. I'm headed to the hospital for a doctor appointment."

Gage pushed back away from the table. "I'll let you two talk. I should probably get back to my computer anyway. I just wanted to run that by you, Iva May."

"Wait just a second," Iva May said, putting a hand on his forearm. "Beverly, Gage was saying that Zoriah might be more interested in opening a second-hand store. I told him that he could have the stuff that I had boxed up for the yard sale. Were you going to sell anything?"

"I wasn't. But I do have a lot of things I need to donate to Goodwill. I can donate them to Zoriah instead."

Gage felt his chest expand with hope. Depending on how much stuff Miss Beverly had, Zoriah might not need anything else.

He tried not to appear too eager. "I know Zoriah would really appreciate that. I talked with her a little bit about canceling the yard sale or asking people to donate their things, but she was completely against it. She didn't want anyone to not make money that they needed in order to survive."

"That sounds like Grandma Heater," Iva May said.

"That sounds like the Zoriah I knew as a child," Beverly added. "I would say, from what I've seen and heard so far since she's come back, that she's grown into a beautiful, kind, and caring woman. I think we ought to put this out to anyone who was thinking about participating in the yard sale."

"I can talk to anyone who comes in the diner. That's not hard. I can even put a sign up, although...?" Iva May lifted her brow and looked at Gage.

"Maybe not. Zoriah was uncomfortable with the idea, but I know she'll go along with it if there's a lot of support. But I know she doesn't want to feel like a charity case." He didn't want to make her feel like one. He was doing this to help her, not to hurt her feelings or make her feel like there was some kind of problem.

He just… There was some kind of connection he felt with Zoriah that he didn't feel with anyone else, hadn't ever felt. And he found himself wanting to do whatever it took to help her and see her smile.

He didn't want her angry or upset, and he didn't want her to decline everything that people might give just because she felt they were forced into it.

But he also thought she probably had no idea the community highly respected her, not just because of her grandmother but because of the way she was before she left town and because of the way she'd been since she came back.

"You can go on back to your apartment, Gage," Iva May said. "Beverly and I can handle this. We'll get together and figure out the people who don't usually come into the diner, and we'll make sure they know. And we won't make anyone feel pressured. There will still be a yard sale, but Zoriah will have enough to stock her store, and it won't be the leftovers." Iva May dusted her hands off as the bell rang and a couple walked in.

The women stood together. Gage took a step toward the door, then stopped.

"I'd heard that Anitra and John were going East because there was a problem with his family. Do you need help here at the diner?" he asked.

Beverly and Iva May looked at each other, then shook their heads.

"I think they're going back for a funeral, but they won't be gone long," Iva May said sadly.

"I hadn't heard."

"We found out this morning, just after breakfast. John got a phone call."

"That's too bad." He made a note to say something to Zoriah and at least send Anitra and John a card. "If I can help, let me know. I worked a few evenings last year, and I didn't burn a single piece of toast."

"That's because you were scrubbing the floors after hours," Iva May said with a look before she swished around her chair and walked to the counter, greeting the couple who was waiting.

"Thanks for your help," Gage said to Beverly, and she nodded and smiled regally.

Hopefully, things would work out. Sometimes when he stuck his nose in where it might not belong, he had a tendency to make things worse instead of better.

Hopefully, that wasn't true in this instance.

Chapter 12

Z oriah sat at the kitchen table and stared at the neat figures of numbers on the notebook in front of her.

She'd crunched the numbers three times, after searching online for various lots of used items.

There was a whole business of buying and selling lots of used things that she'd had no idea about. The contents of storage units, people who cleaned out attics and houses, even people who tore down barns and other old buildings and sold the boards.

She'd come to the conclusion that putting some kind of donation center either out front or at the side of her building would be the best way to get new things for her store, if people would donate.

In the summer, she wouldn't have any trouble. In the winter, she might bid on storage units or even bid on cleaning out attics and cellars.

Mark and Macy might enjoy doing it with her. It could be something they could do as a family, maybe making a business out of it. That might be more than she could handle, and she didn't even know if they would think the idea was great or dumb.

Regardless, it was her job to keep them together as a family. If they didn't like that, they'd come up with something else, because she was going to do everything she could to make sure that even though she was just an aunt, and would never take the place of their mom, and certainly couldn't be a dad, they would have the best and most normal family possible in their circumstances. Beyond normal. She didn't want them ever to doubt that they were loved and accepted and that whatever they did, she would never stop loving them and supporting them.

She also hoped they could have fun together.

High hopes, when she wasn't even sure she was going to be able to pay her bills.

She looked at the list of numbers again. She could probably swing it with her last paycheck, as long as they were very, very frugal. She'd priced out large containers as well, ones that were similar to the collection containers she'd seen outside of other secondhand stores.

She wasn't going to be able to afford one of those right away, but she could at least make a sign and hang it in front of the cash register, announcing that they were accepting donations in the store.

It would be harder, but they could take things to the back and separate them there. They just couldn't accept donations after hours.

She tapped her pencil on the table and tried to think of a place where she could cut corners.

If it were just her, she could eat macaroni and cheese and hot dogs or beans and rice and completely cut out the grocery budget.

But she didn't want the kids to suffer too much.

Although sometimes suffering cemented a bond in a family. If they all had a common purpose, maybe the kids would be willing to eat beans and rice for two weeks, especially if they had the opportunity to start a new business.

If only she could guarantee them that if they made that sacrifice, the business would succeed.

She just couldn't.

Maybe a secondhand store wouldn't be as popular as what she thought it would be in a beach/tourist town.

She heard some clanging and banging from downstairs and figured that Mark and Gage were finishing up. It was a little bit past the time Gage usually left, so she put her pencil down and pushed back on her chair.

Before she could move out of the kitchen, she heard Mark calling, "Aunt Zoriah! There are people out here to see you. They want you to come out."

"I'm coming," she said, glancing at the tablet that lay open on the table.

Maybe she would be inviting people up for tea or coffee. Unlikely, but she grabbed the tablet and put it on top of the refrigerator along with the pencil, just in case, before hurrying out.

She heard voices as she walked down the stairs and turned the corner.

There were more than a few people, some she didn't even recognize, as she walked out. Her eyes opened wider as she figured there were at least twenty people in the empty store.

Iva May stood closest to her with Beverly beside her. They were both smiling, which eased the ball of tangled wire in her chest, somewhat anyway.

Her eyes swept the room again, and she noted Gage in the back, his hands over his chest, his eyes on her.

Just making eye contact with him eased the tightness even more, and she lifted her lips in a little smile which he returned, nodding his head, as though greeting her.

She'd brought sandwiches down, but she'd gone back upstairs to keep working on her numbers and doing her research using her phone, since she still hadn't gotten her internet installed, so they hadn't talked.

She moved a little, her eyes catching on something outside. Iva May was saying something, but Zoriah shifted to try to see the blonde head that stopped. Was that Macy? It looked like the same three people she had seen when she and Gage had been walking along the beach.

The blonde shifted… Macy? She couldn't tell, and she moved to get a better look.

"Zoriah? We all came here because we have something to tell you." Iva May turned toward her, smiling at her and putting an arm around her shoulders as though she was going to need the support for whatever Iva May had to say.

Zoriah tried to smile, but for some reason, she was shaking. She leaned into Iva May. Her arm tightened around her.

"Someone told us that you might be interested in opening a secondhand store rather than an apparel store. That sparked an idea in us." Her arm swept the room, including everyone in it and somehow including the whole town, too. "We all got together and have been talking about this all week. We were going to have a yard sale tomorrow, but if you look at the weather, it's supposed to start raining this evening, and it's going to rain the entire weekend."

"We would be canceling it anyway." Miss Beverly smiled, walking over to Zoriah and putting her hand on her arm gently.

Zoriah didn't say anything. She wasn't sure what to say.

"So we decided, rather than rescheduling the yard sale, we would talk to the community and solicit donations for you to open a secondhand store." Iva May looked over the heads of the people there. "We also had someone, who would like to remain anonymous, offer to buy goods from people who were planning on selling them in order to make ends meet."

"We don't want anyone to go broke because we cancel the yard sale. But we feel like we're doing it for a good cause," Miss Beverly explained.

Zoriah wanted to protest that it was too much, but she didn't want to return this huge, beautiful gesture with scorn or ingratitude.

"We also had someone donate a donation container, and as long as you're agreeable, it will be coming at the beginning of next week and we'll set it up along the side of your building." Bill, who she remembered from her childhood and who still operated the surf shop, stepped forward, his hands in his pockets, his face serious, although there was kindness in his eyes.

He must be fifty, or maybe a little older, and she had heard long ago that there was some tragedy in his past, but he'd been a pillar in the Blueberry Beach community, maybe not providing vocal leadership but always providing that undergirding of support anywhere he was needed.

"I've given the girls off from working at the candy store. Both our daughter, Sierra, and also Naomi and Lexi, for as long as they need to help you organize things and get your store set up if you want them." Adam Coates spoke without moving from the back of the crowd. His arm sat firmly around his wife, Lindy, and his head tilted toward hers. She leaned into him and smiled and nodded at his words.

"Basically, what we're saying is we'll do whatever it takes to get you set up. We want to see your grandmother's store come to life again," Iva May said, squeezing Zoriah, her voice warm and soft.

"If you need a handyman, beyond what Gage can do, someone to help with shelves, or I'm actually not a bad electrician, and I can help you with your internet and anything else you need. Just ask." This was from a man she didn't recognize, who looked to be in his late forties and who stood back with Gage.

He wore a shirt with his name on it, but she couldn't quite read it.

"I'm not sure I know you," she said.

"I'm Ethan. I own the hardware store. I work there too, and if you need me, I live overtop of it. Just knock on the door, I'll open up the store and get whatever you want."

Most of the people in the room were nodding at that, like at one time or another, they'd knocked on his door for whatever reason.

"Thank you," she said, feeling like the words were inadequate but grateful to be able to take care of that one small detail that nagged her, because facing the overwhelming generosity of everyone standing in the room was almost more than she could handle.

"I don't know what to say," she said, looking first at Iva May and then at Beverly like they might help her.

"You don't need to say anything. We're thankful you're here. We're thankful you brought your niece and nephew and that you're opening Grandma Heater's store. It's something we've been hoping would happen, and now that it almost has, we want to give you that final push."

"Not many people choose to return to their hometown and do things that will help out there. A lot of them head to the city and think about ways to help themselves. Our towns would die without people coming back and not just opening up businesses but shopping at those businesses," Adam said and sounded like he knew what he was talking about.

Why wouldn't people come back when they were welcomed like this?

Even with Iva May's arm around her and Beverly's hand on her arm, Zoriah's knees were shaking, and she just couldn't hold herself up anymore.

"I need to sit down," she said softly with weakness in her voice and a tremble caused by the tightness in her throat.

She could not believe the kindness of these relative strangers, and even though she was biting the inside of her cheeks, her eyes filled with tears.

Her hand went to her chest, and she swallowed. She had to find words, but she just...she couldn't think of what to say.

"I'm overwhelmed. I...I never thought that you all would be so kind to me. I mean, I know you knew and loved my gram, but...this is just too much." She looked at the faces that had gathered closer as they looked down at her. "I just can't accept it. I would owe everyone here more than I could ever repay."

Even though they'd provided the solution to all of her problems—how to pay for the inventory, how to collect it—and would enable her to stretch her last paycheck further and longer.

"We want you to," Lindy said, coming forward and kneeling down with her hand on Zoriah's knee. "Not just because we loved your grandmother, although we did. I visited her shop every time we came here for summer vacation, and she was almost like a mother to me. I remember seeing you sitting in the back, doing your schoolwork, working the cash register, or straightening merchandise. I want you in that shop. And I am excited that I can help." She grunted a little. "We moved from Pennsylvania, and I have a ton of stuff in storage. I don't need any of it. I've lived without it for more than a year and barely thought about it. Adam and I are leaving tonight and heading back to Pennsylvania to empty it out. It's all yours."

Chapter 13

Z oriah couldn't help it. Lindy's words made her start crying in earnest. What had she ever done to deserve that kind of a gift? Nothing. She hadn't done anything. Not a thing.

But she could tell from the look on Lindy's face that not only was she not going to take no for an answer, but it would truly make Lindy happy to be able to donate to her shop. She wasn't just saying that, she truly wanted to be able to keep the shop open, and it gave her a good feeling to be donating to that and contributing to the community.

Saying no would not just hurt her feelings, it would make her sad.

Beverly rubbed Zoriah's arm and Iva May still held her tight while she swiped at her tears and looked around the room.

If she said no, she would be letting them all down. Disappointing everyone. It would make them happy to help her, even though she felt overwhelmed and undeserving.

"I'd consider it a personal favor if you would accept," Bill said, seeming to be uncomfortable with her tears, as he shifted from side to side and looked at a spot on the floor to the left of her foot as he spoke.

It made her smile, his classic reaction to her tears.

"I wouldn't want to deny you a personal favor. I don't deserve it, but...okay. Okay," she said, lifting her hands like there was nothing more she could do. "Whatever you guys give me, I'll find a way to set it up in the store, and I'll start selling it. Just know that I know I'll owe each and every one of you."

"You can quit feeling like that, because you don't," Beverly said.

"I finished painting the ceiling tonight. Can they start bringing things to-morrow?" Gage asked, stepping forward from the back where he had been standing.

She nodded, her heart feeling so big and thick like it could burst at any time. He was the one who had started this all. She owed him more than everyone else because he had come up with the idea.

Not that she needed another reason to admire him, or to like him, or to want to spend time with him.

"I'll start telling people when they can expect to start shopping when you have an idea of the date you'll be open," Iva May said, giving her one last squeeze before she straightened, one hand on her back.

"Why couldn't we plan on next Saturday?" Zoriah asked, looking around, wondering if someone could tell her that was feasible or not.

"You told me you had all the permits and everything that you need from the state and you have your business set up with the IRS."

"Gram had all that stuff done already. And I never closed it out. We just made it inactive with the accountant. When I talked to him, he said it wouldn't be hard at all to get it back up and running again. All the forms and accounts are already there."

"There you have it. You can open just as soon as you can get the stuff set up. You probably don't even need to wait until next Saturday," Bill said, sounding a little gruff, but it was a happy gruff.

"I think he's right, although you can give yourself a little bit of breathing room if you plan on Saturday," Lindy said. "I had the candy store ready to open a couple of days before it actually did, and it was nice after the hustle and bustle of getting everything done to just have a couple of days to breathe before I jumped in."

"Then there you go, Iva May. We open next Saturday."

"What are you gonna call it?" someone asked from behind Iva May.

"I don't know." She bit her lip. "Maybe I could talk to the kids about it, and we can see if we can come up with a name that works for all of us. After all, hopefully they'll keep the tradition going and at least let me watch their kids some so we have children running around the store again." The idea made her smile. She hadn't even thought about grandchildren or grandnieces and nephews. Maybe they would call her grandma.

Macy was only seventeen. That was years away. Still, the idea appealed to her.

Speaking of Macy, she looked around and saw that at some point Macy and Naomi and Lexi and Sierra had slipped into the store and were standing over by the door.

She met Macy's silent eyes and smiled.

"Did you hear?" she asked, and people parted when they saw she was looking behind them, so she had an unobscured view of her niece.

"I did. That's amazing." Macy's words and tone were exactly right, but there seemed to be a bit of a shadow in her eyes.

Zoriah's stomach twisted, and she remembered that she'd never asked Macy if it had been her talking to those strange people.

She dismissed it as her overactive imagination or maybe just being paranoid about being responsible for two other humans.

Macy was so good, never doing anything wrong, it had to have been someone else. Not that talking to people in the street was wrong. Just... There was something about those people.

Her eyes went to Mark. He was grinning and had moved over to stand beside Gage.

Gage had his arm around Mark, and although they didn't look anything alike, they could have been father and son just from the way they were standing showing affection and respect to each other.

"Thank you," she said, her eyes still feeling leaky but no longer running over. Her voice at least was stronger. "Thank you guys so much. I really appreciate this and wish that there was something I could do to pay you all back."

"Just having the store open is more than enough for me."

"Me too."

There was a chorus of agreement, and then one by one, they came over to shake Zoriah's hand and walk out.

Zoriah stood as they came by, smiling a watery smile and introducing herself to the few she didn't know, and thanking them, which was all she could think of to do.

Iva May and Beverly stayed for a little longer, chatting and offering to help when she set things up and laid things out, but they refused her invitation to go upstairs for tea and walked out shortly after everyone else did.

That left Gage standing alone, as Mark left with his friend and Macy stood outside the door chatting with Gage's girls and Sierra.

"I don't know what on earth to do with you," she said as he walked toward her.

"How about you say you'll go out with me?"

Her eyes widened, although she was more excited than surprised. "You didn't have to go through these lengths to get me to go out with you." She waved her hand around at the now empty store and indicated all of the things that had transpired this evening.

"Maybe I felt like I did."

"I assure you, you didn't."

He ducked his head down and put a hand in his pocket. "I know. I wanted to. They wanted to. They were so excited and happy to be able to help you, I promise."

"I'm used to earning things. Or at the very least, I'm used to people who expect something in return when they give something to me. This is an overwhelming gift, and it's just so much more than I could ever pay for... I don't even know how to explain it, but it's more than I dreamed of, more than I deserve, and I don't know how to act or what to say."

"Just be you. Just open the store and be you." He stood beside her, and his hand moved like maybe he would touch her, run his hand down her cheek or something, but he didn't. "I think next weekend's going to be really busy for you, maybe we could plan on going out the following Friday night?"

She nodded. "That sounds amazing. I'll definitely be looking forward to it."

"Good. I will be too. I guess I don't have to go out with you in order to enjoy being with you, but I thought it might be something you would like."

"I feel the same. We don't have to go anywhere. We can just sit on chairs on the sidewalk, and I'll be happy."

"Let's do something a little fancier than that."

"Up to you."

They grinned together, and then he looked around. "Everything's painted down here. I'm ready to start upstairs whenever you are. I don't want you to worry about the cost of paint."

"No. I can't have you buying paint for me."

"I'll buy it now, you can pay me back for it, but that way, all the painting will be done. You don't have to if you don't want me upstairs painting. I just figured I'd offer. Not to mention, if I'm here painting, I'll be around if you need a shelf slapped together, or something heavy moved, or help with something else."

"You can be pretty persuasive," she said.

"With certain people, I put a lot of effort into it."

"I see. I'm glad I fit that certain people criteria."

"You're the only one." He grinned, and she wasn't sure exactly what to make of that comment, whether he was teasing or not.

Regardless, they were both grinning as he left, and she tried to keep her heart in her chest and not break out in tears again.

One thing was for sure, she'd be looking for ways to do what she could to help anyone else out, because she owed everyone so much more than she could ever repay.

Chapter 14

"**W**hat if no one comes?" Zoriah said, biting her lip and wringing her fingers together.

"People are going to come," Gage assured her, setting the cordless drill he was holding on the shelf in the back room where Zoriah stood, surrounded by all the things they couldn't fit in the display area. "How could they see your sign – Grandma's Blueberry Boutique – and pass it by?

"Do you think I should turn this into a display area too?" she asked.

They'd already talked about it, and he'd already given her his opinion, but he figured it was her nerves talking, and if it calmed her down for him to say it once more, he would.

"I think you should leave it the way it is for now. And then, as you have time, you can clean out the basement and use the outside stairs to bring things in, and eventually, we'll take everything that's here and either have it in the basement or turn it into a display. But not today."

"All right. I know we already talked about it. I'm sorry I asked again."

"Not a problem. Makes me feel important when you ask for my opinion," he said, winking at her.

"I'm all about making you feel important," she said, and he thought maybe she forgot her nervousness for just a little bit.

"Don't forget, you owe me for everything I'm doing for you."

Her eyes opened wide. "I have to pay you?" she said slowly. Then she shook her head. "Of course. Of course I have to pay you. Just, I hope you don't mind if I don't pay right away?"

"You're paying me next Friday. Our date. Don't tell me you've forgotten?" He put both hands on his heart. "You wound me."

"Oh my goodness. I'm sorry. I should have known you were joking. I guess I'm just not thinking straight right now."

"You're not. And I'm taking advantage of it by teasing you." He leaned his shoulder against the wall and tried to get her to meet his eyes. "I guess I thought it might take your mind off of your nervousness, and your unfounded worries about people not showing up, if you were laughing instead of twisting your hands together and imagining the worst things that could happen."

"I'm sure you're right. I guess… I guess I just can't help it."

"Come on. You're in charge of what goes on up here." He tapped his head. "Aren't you?"

"Yes?"

He laughed. "Don't sound so sure about it. Really, you're supposed to be able to take your thoughts captive, right?"

"I remember that verse."

"Well, do you think we'd be commanded to do something we can't do?"

"I guess not. But sometimes it takes a while to apprehend a fugitive and make them a captive, right?"

He laughed. "That sounds like an excuse."

"I know you're right. I should be able to get a handle on that."

"Well, it's not necessarily that you should. It's just, this is gonna be a lot more fun for you if you don't think about all the terrible things that could possibly happen. So what if they do?"

"What do you mean? If I can't pay the bills, it's going to be a major problem."

"You own the building. You have a car. If your business fails, you could probably get a job at the hospital, right? Or even at the diner? You just need enough to buy food and groceries and pay your taxes."

"True."

"Not that that's what you want to do, but if this fails, there's got to be something else that comes up. You know that whole God closes a door and opens a window thing."

"That's not Bible," she said, sounding sure of herself.

"Busted. But He does promise not to give you more than what you can handle."

"True." She ran her hand over the edge of a jewelry box with a unicorn on the top of it. "I guess I didn't realize until I moved here, but if I think about it, I feel like I'm all alone in the world. You know? Sometimes, your family feels like your safety net. Your mom, your dad, your siblings, your kids, your husband, aunts, uncles, cousins, anyone who, if you fail, they catch you, you know? Like it's embarrassing to move back home to your mother, but at least if you have a mother to move back home to, you've got more than I do."

He hadn't realized that about her. That there really was no one else. No family anyway. How sad. But still, she would be okay.

"Maybe this won't help you, because maybe you just want me to commiserate with you instead of offering solutions?"

"How about you offer me a couple solutions and then commiserate with me? I think that'll be okay."

He chuckled and then lifted his hand, because this wasn't something he told too many people. "You said that about your family, and I understand, I guess as well as I could without having lost all of mine. But you could have a family like mine, who, when you fail, they almost rejoice over it. It's like they're watching for you to fail and even maybe hoping for it."

She gasped, just a little breath, but it was a gasp nonetheless. "That's terrible!"

He nodded. "I know. But it's true." He spread his hands around again, like there was nothing he could do. "I tried so hard to get along with my brother, but it's like everything I do, he can't stand it. He always sees me as the bad person. Always sees everything I do as trying to get ahead of him. I can't want anything, or I'm competitive, I can't have anything good happen to me, or I'm just doing it to show off. I can't be successful, or I'm rubbing it in his face. And it's not even that I'm super successful or any of those things."

"What about your parents?"

"He lives closer to them. He's always telling them that I'm mean to him. I'm competitive with him. That I do all these terrible things to him, and they believe it. I don't know what I can do. Because I wasn't unkind to him to begin with." He shrugged and looked away. He wished he hadn't brought it up. "Never mind. It's hard to explain."

"I understand. I think to myself that people who have families just don't appreciate them, but maybe that's making an assumption on my part that everyone's family wants the best for them."

"I could fail, and you're right, I could move back home with my parents. They still live in the house I grew up in. But the problem is my brother would crow about it and my parents would be unbearable to live with. So there is a safety net, I guess, but it's not too much better than falling into the hands of strangers, which brings me to my second point."

"Go ahead. I'm listening."

She was smiling now and no longer wringing her hands, even if she did look distressed over the state of his family.

It had been embarrassing to admit, but true nonetheless. He was ashamed to tell her that he'd stopped trying. How many years did he have to try and be insulted and put down before he quit?

"Did you see how the town rallied around you to open the store?"

"I did. That's the problem. Everyone expects me to make it a success. What if I don't? What if it becomes a huge, miserable failure? What if nothing I do turns out right?"

"There you go again," he said, putting a hand on her arm and trailing his fingers down it before dropping his hand back to his side. "What if you're a smashing success? What if your store is the most popular store in Blueberry Beach and people come from thousands of miles away to visit you, and you get your own TV show?" He chuckled. "Isn't that the measure of success nowadays?"

"I don't think I want a TV show. I just want enough money that I can raise my niece and nephew and not have them taken from me."

"I think the residents of Blueberry Beach will make sure that that doesn't happen," he said, mostly to reassure her, but then he added, "That's not what I was talking about. See how they all rallied around you? Do you think they wouldn't do that again if the store doesn't take off? Say a secondhand store doesn't work in a beach town. Don't you think the residents will come through for you again? Wouldn't it be better having neighbors and friends who rally around you rather than a family who practically cheers when you screw up?"

"But how do I know that they're going to rally around me again? Maybe they'll be sick of helping me after I mess up twice?"

"Would you get tired of helping someone in town? Last year this time, Anitra needed help at the diner, and everyone pitched in. Again, they're gone for a funeral, and everyone's pitching in." After he left Zoriah's store last night, after helping her set up all the final touches, they had gone and scrubbed the diner together, washing the windows and chairs and disinfecting the countertops in kitchen.

"No, you're right. I wouldn't."

"I thought so. I might need to do it again, if something happens, God forbid, to the baby they have now. Or if something happens to one of them. We're not going to say, too bad. You got help twice, we're not pitching in again. Of course not. Everybody's going to do whatever it takes to help them, no matter what happens. Right?"

"But his sickness is different than financial ruin or difficulty."

"Do you really believe that? Will they say 'her problem isn't the right kind of problem, so I'm not going to help her'?"

"You make me sound silly."

"That's because...it is. Although, I like you, Silly."

"You know, I think I like you too." Her face grew serious. "I really do appreciate all your help."

"She's getting mushy. I can't take it. Is it time to open yet?"

"So, when we go on our date next week," she said, glancing at her phone and holding it up to show that they had four more minutes until nine o'clock. "If you want to spend the evening with me, you'll have to put up with me getting mushy."

"I think you're supposed to get mushy on dates."

"I'm gonna get mushy about this first," she said, adjusting the jewelry box just slightly so that it was exactly parallel to the shelf that it was sitting on.

"So you're saying if I want the other kind of mushy stuff, I have to put up with this kind of mushy stuff?"

"You have to put up with my gratitude. You have to put up with me thanking you. And you definitely have to put up with me asking what I can do to repay you. That's the mushy stuff you have to put up with, if you want any other kind of mushy stuff."

"Well, the mushy stuff is my favorite part of the date, so go ahead. I'll put up with the uncomfortable kind of mushy stuff now."

"Too late. I think we ought to open two minutes early. That will set a good precedent, right?"

"Sure will," he said as he followed her through the door and into the display room where Macy was standing behind the counter at the cash register, doodling on a notebook, while Mark paced back and forth in front of the door.

"Is it time yet?" Mark turned and asked them anxiously when he heard them walk in.

"Almost. We thought we'd open a little early," Zoriah answered.

"Yes!" Mark said. "People have already been walking by and peering in the windows. I think they really love the displays."

Zoriah looked at Gage, and they exchanged a smile. Everyone loved the displays.

"Are you ready, Macy?" Zoriah asked.

"You think anyone's going to come?" Macy asked, and she flipped the pencil between her fingers.

"I have heard, from a very reliable source, that we need to take our thoughts captive and just think about good outcomes, and not worry that bad things are going to happen," Zoriah said, and then she winked at Macy whose lips turned up.

"I suppose those are words of wisdom from Mr. Gage?"

"That's right. Although I got the whole lecture. That was just the condensed version."

"The cliff notes. It's all I need," Macy said flippantly, and he almost thought that maybe he'd been wrong about Macy having an issue, since her smile was so bright. "Bring it on. We're ready. This is going to be a smashing success."

"She's a quick learner," Gage said, winking at Macy.

"I guess I take after my aunt."

Mark had already flipped the sign and stepped away from the door. The bell jingled, and the first customer stepped in.

Chapter 15

"I can't believe how fast the day went," Zoriah said as she turned the closed sign over on the door and leaned against it. Exhausted.

"I thought I would be bored," Macy said. "But it was fun to talk to everyone. They were so friendly. Even people I didn't know."

Macy hadn't been behind the cash register all day, having gone over to Gage's apartment to have a study session with his girls for the majority of the afternoon, but she'd come back and helped them close.

Mark had helped for most of the day but had taken several hours off to be with his friends. He had left after Macy had come back and was still down the street.

"So is this when you're going to tell me I was right?" Gage asked, shoving his hands in his pockets and standing in a big empty spot where there had been a dresser. It sold about forty-five minutes before closing, and they hadn't replaced it with anything.

"About what?" Zoriah asked, confused. "About the price on the dresser?"

"That too. You were going to ask fifty dollars too little for it. I think you could have actually asked a hundred dollars more."

"But I didn't want to ask too much."

"I understand. But no, I was talking about this morning when I told you not to worry. You can go ahead and say I was right now. I'll listen."

"Okay, doofus. You were right. It was silly for me to worry. Especially today." Part of her wanted to say, but what if they don't come back next week? What if no one ever sets foot in the store again? What if it was just an opening-day thing? But she knew those questions were silly. No one could tell. There was no way to know. Still... "I didn't realize that owning a store was so hard."

He laughed. "And you've only done it one day."

"I know! But things are going out so quickly, I couldn't keep the floor stocked with stuff, then people wanted to talk, and I can't sell things if I'm talking to people, and my feet started to hurt, and if you hadn't insisted, I would have totally missed lunch."

"As it was, you didn't eat until three o'clock. I was afraid you were going to pass out on the floor. That might put a damper on business."

"Exactly. We don't want people coming into the store and thinking that the owner can't stay on her feet."

"We could just start a rumor that I knocked you off your feet," he said.

When he grinned at her like that, her heart always flipped over. "Well, I guess it wouldn't be too far from the truth. But maybe I feel like you've knocked a little too hard, if I'm unconscious on the floor."

"Hey. If I have that effect on women..."

She laughed. "Women?"

"Just one. Just want to have that effect on you."

"Guys." Macy shifted behind the cash register. Zoriah had completely forgotten she was there. "Maybe I should leave you two alone."

"You can stay, Macy. Mushy stuff makes him uncomfortable as well."

"Nope. That kind of mushy stuff is okay. When you look at me like that, you could say anything."

"Get a broom and sweep the floor?" she said, teasing, but he grunted.

His laugh was ironic. "Even that." He walked away, grabbing the broom from the back room, and coming out, and sweeping up the sand and debris that had been tracked in during the day.

"I was keeping a tab of how much we had sold, can we add it up?" Zoriah said as she walked over to the counter and leaned down on it, her aching back feeling relief at the change in position.

"Right here," Macy said, turning a notebook to face her.

During breaks between customers, she'd been writing down all sales.

"That's just over one thousand dollars. Do you really think that's right?"

"It is. But I don't think it would have been nearly that much if Ethan hadn't hooked us to the Internet. So many people paid with cards."

"That was a huge blessing that he was able to get that done yesterday." They had all the equipment, they just needed the company to come and hook them up. Ethan was able to get the equipment connected, then he pulled in a favor from someone he knew at the company to get them online. "I can hardly believe it. That is amazing. I know we won't make that much every day, but..." She looked at Macy with wide eyes. "You realize that's pure profit?"

Macy just looked at her blankly.

"We didn't pay anything for the inventory. It was all donated to us, so every penny that we make is profit, other than having to pay things like the internet bill and electricity. But we don't have to pay for any inventory. That's huge."

Macy nodded, chewing on her lips thoughtfully. "Maybe we can stock a few more things that we do have to pay for, eventually," she finally said.

"Like what?"

"I had a few people who asked me if we had drinks, and several others who wanted to buy towels, and several people who asked if we had any books to purchase. I sent them to the diner and the surf shop, but it probably wouldn't hurt to have a cooler with cold drinks. The towels I don't know about, but if we don't buy books, maybe we can scrounge up some used ones. I think it was mostly the moms who probably wanted something to do while the kids were playing on the beach."

"Good thinking."

"There are a few other things that people asked for, but…" She twisted the pen in her hand thoughtfully. "Maybe I should keep a list of those things people ask for, just kind of impulse items. You know, like convenience stores have at the checkout counter."

Macy sounded a little insecure, like she wasn't sure with her age and just being a teenager and everything whether she should be making suggestions about their business or not.

Zoriah wanted to encourage her, because she wanted it to be a family affair. Plus, they were good ideas. "I think that's excellent. I'd really love to do that. Both keep a list, and maybe we can get Gage or Ethan to make some shelves here in front. We can keep those things you just mentioned right here where people can grab them." She smiled at Macy. "Thank you so much. I love that you're thinking about things that will help us. And I really appreciate your help today. I don't think we'll normally be that busy, but it was a huge blessing to have you here."

Macy beamed, and she gave an almost embarrassed smile. "I really had fun. I suppose it'll get old, but I enjoyed it."

"I say we go over to the ice-cream shop, and I'll treat everyone to some ice cream. I think after today, we deserve it." Gage came over with the dustpan full of dirt and holding the broom.

"I think maybe I should be the one treating everyone to ice cream. I think after the day we had, I can afford it."

Gage opened his mouth, and she thought he was going to protest, but then he looked at her, and it was almost like he realized how much this meant to her. He nodded. "I don't think I've ever had anyone take me out for ice cream before. I think I'll let you."

"That's good." Her eyes caught on his for a second, and her stomach looped. She needed to thank him, not just for what he did today but for coming up with the idea and turning it into a reality. But he wouldn't appreciate it now. She tore her eyes away and turned toward Macy. "Are you ready?"

"If you don't mind, I'm tired. Maybe I'll go lie down for a little bit."

That seemed odd. Zoriah's eyes skimmed over Macy. "You're not sick?"

"No. I guess I'm just not used to being on my feet all day."

"Okay." It still didn't seem right, but she wouldn't argue. She felt exhausted too, but maybe it was the idea of going out with Gage, even just for ice cream, that had given her a second wind. She felt like she could do anything, goodness, she could find the energy to roller-skate, or go for a hike, if Gage were going to go along. "We won't be gone long."

"Enjoy yourself, Aunt Zoriah. You deserve it." Macy smiled, and Zoriah nodded.

"Thanks."

Zoriah turned. Gage held out his hand. She smiled at him as her hand slipped into his. It felt perfect.

Chapter 16

"I'm nervous," Gage said as Zoriah put her hand in his and he helped her out of his car.

Maybe he shouldn't admit it. Nervousness was not an appealing characteristic in a man, but it didn't seem to bother Zoriah. In fact, if anything, it made her smile.

"Why?" she asked, softly and a little shyly, like she was nervous, too.

"We spent so much time together painting in your store and eating and talking. I thought I was completely comfortable with you. But..." He looked at the upscale restaurant they were about to enter, unsure how to explain what the issue was.

"I'm sorry. I don't mean to make you uncomfortable."

He shook his head. "See? I'm so nervous I'm not even saying what I really want to say." He closed her door but didn't move, standing and facing her with her hand clasped between them.

"It's not you that makes me nervous, I just... I can't remember the last time I wanted a date to go well as badly as I want this one to." He knew what that meant—he really cared what Zoriah thought. If he wasn't nervous, it would indicate that he didn't care.

"Same for me. Maybe it's because of us already talking and knowing each other, but I know I want to know you more. And I suppose there's always that fear that what I want isn't going to be what you want, and it won't work out."

She could not have said his words any better. "I guess you don't have to worry about that with me. I want us to work out."

"Even if I eat three times as much as you do? And drop my dessert on the floor? And get toilet paper stuck to my shoe while I'm in the restroom and spend the rest of our evening dragging a trail of white stuff around with me?"

He lifted a shoulder. "You haven't scared me yet. None of that will bother me. Although, if you spend the entire evening complaining about your hairstylist, or yell at the waitress, or slap my fingers when I go to steal the black olives off your plate, that might make a difference." He grinned.

"I hope you're kidding about that last one because I like black olives."

"Oh. So I'll have to be sneaky about that," he said, and her eyes twinkled.

"You sure will. Or maybe I'll get yours first."

"I promise I won't slap your fingers. But I can't promise I won't spend the rest of the meal holding your hand."

"Oh?" Her eyebrows went up, and she looked interested. "So, if I want you to hold my hand, I'll just attempt to steal your olives and pretend to be sneaky, but actually I'll try to get caught." She put her free hand on her waist, her brows lifted in question.

"Exactly. All of that is code for 'I really like you, and I want to hold your hand.'"

"Why couldn't I just say, 'I really like you, and I want to hold your hand?'"

"That would work too."

"I really like you, and I want to hold your hand." Her lip tilted up, and then she looked at their joined hands. "But I think we're already doing that."

"True, but now I know you want to."

He didn't really want to go into the restaurant. Even though they had a beautiful patio, with potted plants and a waterfall, and it was a gorgeous evening, just the right temperature to sit outside under the stars with twinkle lights all around and eat with a woman who had become very special to him.

He supposed it was okay, but if it were him, he'd rather grill steak and sit on his own patio and hold hands and watch the stars and their sparkling reflection on Lake Michigan, and eventually walk on the beach.

The problem was he didn't have a patio, he didn't have a grill, and he didn't have a house.

For the first time since he moved to Blueberry Beach, he had seriously considered looking around for one. It was just so convenient living right on the main street, right by the shops, right by the beach, right in the middle of everything. The girls didn't have to travel to go to work. They just walked down the stairs. They didn't have to travel to play in the beach band except...there was no more beach band.

He tugged on her hand, and they started walking to the restaurant.

"It's too bad the beach band dispersed right after you came. I understand Macy's a pretty good musician, and the girls really had a great time with it."

"I've been thinking about that," she said, and he turned to look at her, an odd note in her voice signaling something was up. "I worked as a nurse, an LPN, but my first degree is in music. Music education. I've never used it, but I do believe I could probably work something up and possibly take charge of it. But being that I'm a newcomer..."

"I don't care. And I don't think anyone else will, either. The beach band was incredibly popular with the tourists last year. The kids and adults who played in it made a good bit of money."

She bit her lip.

He continued. "Don't be scared or intimidated. It wasn't anything that was rigidly organized. Some kids started playing together, and then Mrs. Hershey took over, taking the band to the point where they sounded terrific. People actually stood on the beach, sometimes quite a crowd, and listened to them."

"I'd love to see the music they used. I understand that she wrote the parts for the instruments that she had. I think I could do that."

"My girls, and Sierra, Lindy and Adam's daughter, are three of the members. Macy would make four, and I'm sure they can talk to the kids at school that were in it before, and I can talk to the adults, and we can start it back up again. You just need to figure out when it would suit you."

"You know the adults in it?" she asked.

"Well... I played the trombone. Not all the time, and not very well," he hastened to add, feeling a little embarrassed. After all, she had a music degree, and he was just an amateur. All the lessons he'd had had been in high school. He hadn't even played in college.

"Really?" She looked at him, and the excitement and admiration on her face made his chest swell.

"I'm telling you, not well."

"It doesn't matter. Anyone can practice. If you can read music, you can get better."

"I read music, but mostly Mrs. Hershey had me playing quarter notes keeping the beat. You get too tricky on the rhythm, and I get a little lost." He figured he might as well be honest so she didn't go writing him music that was way over his head.

"That's perfect. I'd really love to hear you guys."

"I'm sure I can get everyone together. It was a labor of love, and I think they're itching to get back to it. Everyone was bummed, especially with the start of beach season getting closer, and knowing how much money we all made last year."

They walked into the restaurant and gave their names so the maître d' could confirm their reservations.

They were soon seated on the patio, settling down and looking at their menus.

"It's beautiful out here," Zoriah said.

"I've actually never been here. I just heard it's the best restaurant on this side of Michigan north of Chicago, and the pictures online are gorgeous. I thought you might like it."

"Who doesn't love beautiful things?"

Maybe his face looked a little guilty, because she tilted her head and looked at him. "You?"

He lifted a shoulder. "I guess I do. But I suppose if I were choosing restaurants, I would choose something with less pressure." That wasn't quite the word he meant.

"Not so fancy? So....you feel like everything you do has to be perfect here?"

He nodded. "Sure. Unless the food's really good. And then the pressure's worth it."

"Okay. I'll agree with that. If the food's not good, the atmosphere isn't worth it. But I do like the beauty, and it's nice to get dressed up and go out once in a while. I wouldn't want to do this every weekend though. It's too formal."

"Once a year?" he asked, thinking that was probably more than enough for him.

"Maybe less. Let's taste the food first."

The waitress came back with their drinks and took their orders. Once she left, Gage put his hand on the table, palm up.

She didn't need to look at it for more than a second or two before her hand slipped into his, and they smiled together.

"I don't want to scare you, but I'm not really interested in casual dating." There. Maybe that conversation was too heavy for a first date. But if they weren't going to be in agreement, there wasn't much point in there being a second date. As much as he wanted it.

But she agreed right away, nodding. "Me either. I'm actually not big on dating at all. I told you I had two long-term relationships that ended up going nowhere. I guess I gave up after that. There didn't seem to be much point in investing so much of myself into a relationship that wasn't going anywhere."

"You didn't want marriage and children?"

"No, that's the problem. I did. But I couldn't find anyone who wanted the same things. And I wasn't interested in going out and just having a good time with men who seemed so stuffy." She looked like she just realized something. "Maybe I'm too stuffy?"

"I don't think so. You should go after what you want. But you probably also didn't have a whole lot of time. Didn't you say you lost your sister and your parents in a short time?"

"Yeah. And before that, I was taking care of my sister and helping her with Macy and Mark."

"That makes sense to me, that you didn't have time to waste on dates that went nowhere."

"You said you moved to Blueberry Beach after your divorce. You didn't live here together?" It seemed like a casual question, but she used one finger to move her spoon, angling it just perfectly with her knife, and he thought maybe she was more interested in the answer than she wanted to let on.

He liked that. He wanted to tell her that he liked that she showed interest in him, but he didn't want to make assumptions that weren't accurate.

"No. We lived closer to Chicago. And she really liked the city and fancy things like this. There's nothing wrong with that," he hastened to add. "The problem was she thought married life was boring. Which I suppose it is. You're with one person all the time, and you kind of get used to each other and maybe start taking each other for granted."

"I think that's true in any long-term relationship," she said, seeming more relaxed and listening intently. It made him feel like she was interested. So many times, his wife hadn't seemed to pay attention to what he said.

"You got custody. That's kind of odd," she said, and it seemed like a question.

"It is. She didn't want them. She left me for her personal trainer, and she hasn't spent more than a few days each year with them since. She's just not interested, which is fine with me. I suppose I would rather it be this way than me constantly fighting for custody, but...I know it hurts the girls. They feel like since their mother doesn't want them, there's something wrong with them. It doesn't seem to matter how many times I tell them that's not true, and it doesn't matter what she says. Of course, when she says she cares about them and then doesn't see them for six or eight or ten months, and doesn't call, doesn't contact them, I guess it rings a little hollow."

"Yes. I would imagine it does. That's too bad, because your girls seem so sweet and nice."

"They're teens, but yeah, I guess I'm kind of partial to them, and if you give me enough time, I'll bore you to death bragging about them."

"I like that. I like a father who loves his girls and will brag about them."

The food came, and as the waitress set it down, they looked at each other and smiled. It smelled delicious, and he could almost read in her eyes that she was thinking that maybe the restaurant would be worth it.

It turned out to be accurate, since the food was some of the best he'd ever eaten, but maybe that was the company. He couldn't recall a meal where he'd had a better time. He couldn't recall being with someone that he liked more than he liked Zoriah.

Both of them were too full for dessert, but violins had been playing in the background, sweet and soft, and after the waitress had set the bill on the table and walked away, he squeezed Zoriah's hand.

"Would you like to dance?" He could hardly believe he'd said it. He wasn't the kind of man who got up in a restaurant and danced, but with Zoriah, he wanted to. Maybe it was just to be able to hold her. Regardless, after her surprised look faded, she nodded.

"I'd love to."

Chapter 17

Z oriah had never in her life danced in a restaurant with a man. She couldn't imagine it was even something she wanted to do. But she also never lingered for three hours over a meal with anyone either.

"I can't believe how time has flown," she said as she got up and followed him over to what wasn't exactly a dance floor but was a little bit open with plants up on both sides and a trellis overhead with some greenery dripping down.

He looked at his watch and huffed. "I had no idea we'd been talking for almost three hours." He stopped and looked at her with concern. "Do you need to get back? I'm sorry, I didn't realize how late it was."

"No, the kids were fine. Mark was staying with his friend up the street, and Macy told me she was going to be with some friends from school before she went home and did her homework. She texted me a while ago and said she was back but that she was going to take a walk along the beach. I thought that the beach was deserted enough this time of year that she would be okay, but I've been thinking about getting a dog."

"I think that's an excellent idea. I love walking on the beach at night, and I let my girls do it, because Blueberry Beach is such a small, safe town, but there's always that thought in the back of my head that something could happen."

She nodded, loving that he knew exactly what she was talking about and cared for his girls as much as she did. "It should scare me how perfect you are."

"Just don't take your rose-colored glasses off, because I'm not."

"I guess I just don't see it."

"Please don't make me tell you all the things that are wrong with me. Not tonight."

"No way. I wouldn't want to have to tell you all the things that are wrong with me in return."

His hands had settled on her waist, and they felt perfect, warm and strong and like she could depend on them. Her hand slipped around his neck. She didn't step closer to him and press against him, even though she wanted to. She had no idea what the rules were for dancing in a restaurant. Not to mention, she didn't want to ruin the sweet companionship that had settled between them.

They talked some more, laughing and enjoying each other's company, until they fell silent and danced long enough that she lost track of time again and was shocked when Gage whispered in her ear, "I guess we better go, they're closing the place down."

She looked around and couldn't believe that there was not a single other person in the restaurant.

"I'm sorry. I lost track of time yet again." She'd never done this before in her life. There had been a lot of dates where she couldn't wait for them to end. She'd been on more where she'd been bored, sitting with the person she'd been with for years as he stared past her shoulder, looking at all the other interesting girls in the restaurant and not paying attention to the one across from him.

Maybe she should not have stayed with someone like that, but when she committed to a relationship, she didn't uncommit easily, and it seemed a small thing to put up with and one that many ladies had to.

But having experienced all those horrible dates, it was a real treasure to be on a date with someone she liked who was fun and who seemed to like her and prefer her over anyone else in the room.

"Is it terrible that I don't want tonight to end?" she asked softly.

He lifted his face enough that he could look into her eyes, and he shook his head slowly.

"Me either," he said as he slowly stopped swaying to the music.

Her breath caught, and she moved closer without really meaning to. Her lungs seemed to stop while her heart skittered. Her thumb brushed against the hair at the nape of his neck.

His head lowered, and hers angled up to meet him. Her eyes dropped closed, and there was just a breath between them when a shrill ring startled them both.

They didn't exactly jerk apart, but her eyes flew open and they both moved back a fraction of an inch. His brows raised. "Yours?"

She nodded, knowing it was late and she should get it but fighting the disappointment that pulled under her ribs and still trying to bring herself back to reality.

"I need to get it."

He nodded. "Hopefully, it's just one of the kids wondering where you are," he said, although his voice held an undercurrent of concern, which she shared.

Phone calls in the middle of the night were never good.

Zoriah's heart felt like it was going to skydive out of her chest, and her hands had started to sweat as they dropped from around Gage's neck and she walked over to her purse which still lay on her chair, digging out her phone and fumbling to answer it. Her hands became much more clumsy when she saw the caller ID: Michigan State Police.

She lifted terrified eyes to Gage, who closed the distance between them, his brows furrowed as he put his arm around her and leaned over, looking at her phone.

She didn't know whether he saw the name or not before she swiped and put it to her ear.

"Hello?" Her voice didn't sound like hers. She'd gone from having the most romantic evening of her life to being more scared than she could ever remember being.

What if something had happened to Mark? He said he was spending the night with a friend, but maybe he'd lied to her and was doing something he shouldn't have been. Or maybe they had gotten into something, and he'd gotten hurt.

A million thoughts, none of them good, went through her mind before the voice on the other end said, "This is Officer Weaver of the Michigan State Police force. Is this Zoriah Gibbony?"

"It is." There was still a huge tremble in her voice, and it felt like she was trying to talk underwater.

"You're the guardian for Macy Butler?" the man continued in a businesslike tone.

Her stomach dropped, and she fumbled with the chair, dropping into it while clutching the phone to her ear.

"I am. What happened? Is she okay? Are you at the hospital?" She couldn't bring herself to ask if she had died, if they were in the morgue, or any of the other million morbid questions in her head. The hospital was bad enough.

She couldn't let anything happen to her niece and nephew. They were the only family she had left, and she loved them beyond words. Not to mention she'd be letting her sister down, her parents down, her grandmother down, everyone, they were all depending on her to do this by herself. Raise these children, the last of their family.

"Do you know what your niece was doing this evening?" the man asked.

"Well..." He hadn't answered any of her questions, and she didn't want to answer his. She wanted to ask all of hers again and demand that he answer her. To at least find out if Macy was okay.

But she racked her brain, trying to remember what exactly she'd said to Macy. "She was going to hang out with some friends, get schoolwork done. And then go to our apartment and work there. She said she might take a walk on the beach—did someone hurt her?"

She'd never heard of anyone being assaulted in Blueberry Beach or the Blueberry Beach area, but she closed her eyes, sick with herself. She should not have allowed Macy to go alone. She should have said she had to have someone with her. Why had she been such a terrible parent?

"She's fine. She's in police custody at the Blueberry Beach jail. She's a minor, so we called to let you know where she was. The judge will set bail on Monday morning, and if you post it, you can get her out then."

"She's not hurt?" Zoriah said, slowly processing the officer's words.

"She's not hurt, and I don't think she hurt anyone with her alleged actions of this evening, which is a very good thing."

"Can I talk to her?"

"She's allowed one phone call. She hasn't said who she wants to call yet."

"Can I come see her?"

"Visiting hours are from nine to five Monday through Friday," the officer said in a severe tone, then he softened. "But I'll be on duty starting at two o'clock tomorrow, if you want to come in then and see her for a few minutes."

"Thank you," Zoriah said, unsure and too shocked to think of anything else.

"Have a nice evening, ma'am," the officer said, and then he hung up.

It took a while for Zoriah's hand to slowly lower from her ear and land in her lap.

"How can I help?" Gage asked, going down on one knee beside her, both of his hands closing around hers which were clutching her phone and ice cold. "Tell me what I can do."

She closed her eyes and shook her head, reality setting in as her throat closed, tightened, squeezing, hurting, and the world seemed to shift and rock.

"That was...the police," she said, her voice still holding threads of disbelief. She'd never spoken to the police on the phone before.

So that's what it was like.

Her thoughts were wooden, not making any sense.

Her eyes lifted. Gage knelt in front of her, so earnest, so desirous to help, but she didn't even know what to tell him, didn't know what to do herself.

"Ma'am? Sir? We're closing," a man said, putting a hand on Zoriah's shoulder which she barely felt. "You two were really cute this evening. We enjoyed watching you," the man said softly.

"I'm sorry if we kept you too late. Thanks for letting us stay," Gage said, still sounding like tonight had been the best night of his life, when it had crashed in fiery pieces of flaming metal around Zoriah not even five minutes ago. It had gone from being the best night of her life to the worst.

Somehow, Gage tugged on her hand and managed to get everything together and get them out to the car, enabling the restaurant's workers to clean up and go home.

"Are you ready to tell me?" he asked again.

Zoriah put a hand to her temple, like that would get her brain to start functioning. "I'm sorry. I'm sorry. I...I don't know what to say."

"Who was on the phone?" Gage asked in a reasonable tone.

She swallowed, the movement hurting. "It was the police."

"Did someone die?" he asked in the same caring and low tone. Just trying to get information out of her and maybe calm her with his voice.

"No."

"Was there an accident?"

"I don't know!" She raised her eyes to his, looking at him across the console, as they sat the parking lot. "I don't know! He didn't tell me."

"What did he say?" Gage asked, his tone almost like he was talking to a child.

"He said Macy was in jail!" she almost wailed.

"In jail? Macy?" Gage said, his voice holding disbelief, which made her stomach spin even worse.

She nodded frantically. "What do I do?"

"We'll go to the jail and get her out," Gage said, starting the car and putting it in gear before she could speak.

"But he said the judge wouldn't set bail until Monday."

"Okay. So she's going to call you?" he asked, and she realized he must have been figuring out and putting pieces together of the bits and fragments he'd heard of their conversation.

She nodded.

"Okay. We'll wait on that. In the meantime, let's go home. We'll make sure Mark is okay, and...I think I'd like to check on Naomi and Lexi, since they had been going to be with Macy tonight some."

They drove home in silence, Zoriah's hands twisting along with her stomach and her heart. Her whole body felt tight and uncomfortable.

She had so many questions, but none that were going to get answered. Not tonight. She didn't know how to get the answers. Maybe Mark would know something, but she hadn't thought to text him until they were pulling down Main Street.

Police lights flashed everywhere as officers swarmed both sides of the street, talking to people, conversing with themselves, and putting up yellow tape over broken storefronts as her friends and neighbors swept up glass or huddled together, their heads bent together, like they were whispering.

The street was blocked off, so Gage drove around the back alley and parked behind her building.

Neither one of them had said anything, but she supposed they were both thinking the same thing.

Macy was in jail. Their street was a mess. There were police everywhere. Was Macy responsible for the mess out there?

After he parked the car, Gage grabbed his latch and shoved his door open, while she didn't move.

"Are you coming? Let's find out what's going on."

"I'm scared."

She wanted to know. She wanted to know with all her heart. But mostly she just wanted to know that Macy and Mark were okay. That no one else was hurt, and that Macy had nothing to do with this. She had a feeling that last one wasn't something that she was going to find out when she walked down the alley and talked to her neighbors.

"Do you want me to go find out for you? You can sit here, and I'll come back and let you know." He moved a little, but she shook her head, raising her hand and putting it on the latch.

"No. I need to go. I just... I'm just scared." Her voice cracked, and the tears she hadn't even realized she was holding tried to pour out of her eyes.

She gritted her teeth and fought them back. She couldn't go out in the street bawling and sobbing before she even knew what was going on.

"Are you sure? Because I can get the news and bring it back to you. Whatever it is, I'll be here." He put a hand on her arm and leaned his head down until she met his eyes. "I'm with you. We're going to face this together. You and me."

His words were all the right words, everything she wanted to hear, but she couldn't believe it.

If her niece had anything to do with the mess that she'd just seen on the street where they both lived, where their friends and neighbors and the people who had just helped her open her store all had their livelihoods, if her niece had anything to do with that, Gage wasn't going to want to have anything to do with her. She was sure of it.

But she didn't say that. Instead, she bit her lips, pulling them in and squeezing until blood flowed and the pain in her lips was worse than the pain in the back of her throat from keeping her tears from coursing down her cheeks.

"I'm sure." She took a deep breath, fortifying herself. She had to face this, whatever it was. "I'm ready." She pulled the door latch, and Gage's hand slipped off her arm as she got out.

She couldn't look at him as she put one foot in front of the other and walked out toward Blueberry Beach's main street and the destruction that awaited her.

Chapter 18

Zoriah walked out from between the diner and the candle shop onto a scene like she'd never witnessed in her life. Never thought to witness, especially in Blueberry Beach.

It must have happened a while ago, at least several hours, since the police seemed to be questioning people but not stopping anyone.

She recognized Bill sweeping up the glass in front of his store as Anitra and Iva May along with Lindy and Beverly stood in a group, their heads still bent together, like they were talking low and soft.

Gage wanted to stand beside her, but she couldn't let him. She couldn't let him be associated with her if this was her responsibility in any way.

"I'm going to go talk to the ladies," she said, not feeling quite brave enough to approach a policeman.

There was hurt in his eyes, it couldn't be anything else, but he nodded. "Please don't leave without me," he said, his words a plea, his eyes begging.

She nodded. She didn't have anywhere to go, beside her store.

Her store!

She wanted to yank her head around, but her eyes caught on the other side of the street, and they moved down each storefront. Broken glass, broken windows, the surf shop had merchandise strewn out in front of it, which Bill had been sweeping around. The ice-cream parlor's big, beautifully decorated window, with Blueberry Beach Ice Cream stenciled on it with all the colors of the rainbow, was completely gone, although there was no glass on the sidewalk in front of it, so maybe Bill had already swept that up, or someone else. She didn't know.

The coolers were open, the ice cream melted in puddles, the big two and a half gallon cans strewn around the street. Each storefront on that side of street was completely vandalized, spray paint on the doors. Every second she looked, it seemed worse and worse.

Both windows in the diner were gone, the hardware store, the candle shop, the tires of the bikes on the rack slashed... She felt sick, and she put both hands over her stomach, clenching it tight, as premonition overtook her, and she finally allowed her eyes to land on her shop.

It was perfect.

Not a crack in the glass, the door still closed, no spray paint. It looked serene and beautiful, with her grandmother's decorations still running in the windows.

She'd made it to the group of ladies, but now she wished she hadn't. She wanted to throw up.

Maybe it was her imagination, but it felt like they quit talking and looked at her with disdain.

That couldn't have been because Iva May stepped forward, her arms spreading wide. "Zoriah, it's so good to see you."

Her arms wrapped around her, and her yeasty coffee scent drifted around like a sweet prayer, and Zoriah laid her head on her shoulder, the tears that had been threatening ever since the phone call falling silently as she clung to the older lady and said between gasps of breath, "What happened?"

"Oh, you poor dear. You don't even know." Iva May's hand stroked her hair, and another hand touched her back as Anitra stepped forward, her baby in one arm, her other hand around Zoriah as Lindy came to her other side, and then all the ladies gathered around her, touching her and murmuring.

Finally, she lifted her head and stepped back, not wanting to but needing to know. "What happened?"

The ladies all looked at each other, like they weren't sure who was going to speak.

Finally, Beverly stepped forward, putting her hand on Zoriah's arm. "A group of kids with baseball bats and masks ripped through town, and you can see—they broke the windows and destroyed much of the insides. We want to try to figure out what is salvageable, but the police are looking for clues, and they won't let us in."

"Macy?"

Iva May nodded. "I'm sorry. She was the only one who got caught. I think there were at least two others, but we haven't been told, and as far as I know, they're still running around."

"They said I couldn't go to the jail and get her out," Zoriah said, wishing, even with the disaster that was around her, that she could be with her niece. Find out why she did this. What was she thinking?

"I'm not entirely sure, but I think she might be facing some felonies. Someone had a gun. And there was a tourist on the street who was assaulted. And they were driving a stolen car. I heard someone say drugs."

Zoriah had thought things couldn't get any worse. But she'd been wrong.

"Is she okay?" she asked, fear tightening like sharp claws around her neck.

"Yes," Iva May said simply.

Zoriah bent her head, ashamed. Her niece was fine – but she thought about all the work that the people in front of her had put into helping her open her store. All the things they'd given her, the time they donated, the money she made because of them, how they'd welcomed her with open arms, and her sister's children, and this is what they got for their generosity and kindness.

They should be angry at her. At the very least, they should not be talking to her.

But everyone she looked at, while their eyes might be bloodshot and their cheeks wet, there was no rancor in their gaze.

"I'm so sorry. So very sorry." She didn't know what else to say. She couldn't fix this. Couldn't undo it. But she could... "I'll have to move. I can't have—"

"No!" their voices chorused, all of the ladies speaking, with Lindy putting a hand on her arm to stop her from moving back.

"After what Macy's been through—I'm not saying this is justified, of course it's not. And she'll have to face the consequences. I don't think anyone here is going to pretend that this hasn't been a huge blow to them, their families, their incomes, but Macy is a troubled youth, and we are not going to kick you out or turn our backs on you, or her, just because she's done something terrible."

It was too good to be true. Surely once they thought about it, once they slept on it, once they spoke to their husbands, who had to be angry and upset and scared and wanting to punish Macy to the fullest extent of the law, once the sun rose tomorrow, they would change their minds. They had to.

But she couldn't call them liars. Zoriah was sure they meant exactly what they said right now. Just...probably not once they thought about it.

"Thank you," she said. She stood for a little longer, until she saw Mark and his friend and his friend's father, Ethan, walk up to Gage. She excused herself from the group, saying the words that were necessary, before she walked over.

She felt like she was going through the motions, in a dreamlike state, although she did have the foresight to make sure that everyone had a secure place to stay for the evening, offering her apartment, but everyone declined. They all had locks on their apartment doors, and none of those had been messed with.

And when everyone started to disperse, deciding to wait until morning to pick things up, she went home to her apartment, sending Gage a text after she had walked in, unable to face even one more person she had let down.

She had heard a lot of conversations about insurance, and police investigations, and time, and opening before beach season started, but her brain had been mush, and she wasn't sure that anyone really knew what the morning would bring.

After making sure Mark was okay and talking softly to him for a bit, she lay down on her bed, on top of the covers, and let her tears fall into the pillow, ignoring the text on her phone from the man she'd spent the evening with.

Chapter 19

Gage had been able to pick up a lot more information than he probably should have the night before.

Cooper Sparks had been his gym partner for a while years ago when he worked the night shift and they could go during the day together while Gage's girls were at school.

Cooper was now a state trooper. He hadn't told Gage anything that was strictly confidential, but Gage felt like he had a little more of the inside scoop.

Not that it mattered, since Zoriah seemed to have frozen him out and wasn't talking to him.

He was pretty sure it wasn't because she was upset with him, but more because she was embarrassed at what her charge had done and didn't think that he would want to stay with her.

He had to admit, as he looked at his girls across the breakfast table, listlessly stirring their oatmeal, that he wasn't sure whether he was making the right decision.

Maybe he should back off. She evidently wanted to. Maybe he should allow it.

After all, his girls were becoming very good friends with Macy.

"Dad, what I just can't get over is that I didn't have any idea that Macy was doing these kinds of things," Naomi said, her red-rimmed eyes looking at him, pleading almost, as though wanting him to make sense out of everything for her.

He couldn't.

"You mean this isn't her first time?" he asked, having not known that.

Naomi shrugged a shoulder and looked back down at her oatmeal. "I just heard from some of my friends on social media that she'd been hanging out with this crowd since they moved in. They think there are drugs involved too."

That was information he'd heard. Along with the stolen car and someone being assaulted.

Macy was in some deep trouble. Cooper had been sure she would be facing prison time, unless her age saved her. Which, since she was very close to turning eighteen, it might not.

"I think sometimes when you get caught up with the wrong people, and... She lost a lot of her family in a short amount of time..." He wasn't sure. Sometimes, people felt like they could get away with things. Sometimes, people looked like they were handling hard things like the death of their mother and moving and all the other things that Macy had faced okay. But inside, they just crashed.

He'd gotten that feeling from her, and now he wished he'd pushed harder. But his thoughts had seemed baseless at the time.

"What's going to happen to her?" Lexi asked, not looking quite as torn up as Naomi did, but she was younger.

"I think on Monday we'll be able to bail her out of jail, and then it's just a matter of what charges they bring against her, and I'm not sure exactly." He'd never been involved in anything like this. He didn't really know how the justice system worked, because he'd always stayed on the right side of the law. And thankfully, his girls had too.

"Dad?" Naomi said, her voice having a thread of steel in it, like she was gathering up her nerve and wanted to say something important.

"Yeah, sweetie?"

"I was lying in bed last night, thinking, and at first, I was really angry at what Macy had done. Because I work at the ice-cream shop, and she knows it, and she had to know when she was breaking the windows and destroying the shop that...she was destroying something I loved."

"I think that's a natural feeling," he said, wanting to say more. Wanting to say that you have to get past your anger, because that's the first feeling, but it's not the feeling that's right.

Not that they weren't justified in their anger. Just, anger couldn't be how they lived their lives. Not if they wanted to be different. Not if they wanted to live the ideals they claimed to believe.

"But as I thought about it, I thought that's probably how everyone's going to react. They're going to be mad at her. Because she's taken away so much from our town."

He agreed with that too. It wasn't just the property she destroyed, it was...that elusive sense of security and community that she had taken the metaphorical baseball bat and destroyed. Her friends and her. How long would it be until they could walk down the street without being afraid?

How many of the shop owners would be putting security systems in, when no one, not a single shop owner, had had an electronic security system.

Now it seemed necessary.

He'd considered something stronger for his apartment last night as he lay in bed. Something beyond the simple doorknob lock. A deadbolt at least.

"But..." And here, Naomi bit her tongue and looked at him. "That's not the way I've been taught to react to things."

He blinked. That statement alone was more mature, far more mature than he'd been, even in his twenties and thirties when he'd been married. When someone did something so egregiously wrong, it felt like they deserved his anger.

Thinking back on his interactions with his wife, he'd couldn't remember once, not one time, that she had done something unkind to him and his reaction had gone beyond anything but the anger.

He waited, because Naomi wasn't finished.

"I realized I'm supposed to forgive, and I'm supposed to love her anyway. If I want to be a good friend, if I want to be the kind of friend who stands beside someone when hard things happen to them, then...that's what I need to do."

Gage put both elbows on the table and folded his hands together, putting his chin on top of them.

He hadn't expected that kind of maturity out of his girls.

How could he admit he hadn't decided what he was going to do? He couldn't make his decision based on his relationship with Zoriah. He had to make his decision based on what was best for his girls.

But he'd be lying if he hadn't thought, pretty much all night, about what forbidding his girls to talk to Macy anymore would do to his relationship with Zoriah.

It would destroy it.

How could he date Macy's aunt when his girls weren't allowed to talk to Macy?

But was telling his girls they couldn't talk to Macy or hang out with her the right response?

"I guess what I'm saying is..." Naomi looked up from her bowl, facing him square in the eye. "I want to keep being friends with Macy. And I'm afraid that you're going to tell me I'm not allowed."

He took a breath, letting it flow out, letting the silence come down on the kitchen.

The orange walls, the white cupboards, the stainless steel refrigerator that he'd splurged on and loved, the girls, bigger now than they used to be but still looking to him for guidance, still respecting him, still trying to do right, even if sometimes they did make mistakes and mess up.

He didn't want to lose it. He didn't want to risk it.

"You have a tendency to become like the people you hang around. If you...hang around with people who take baseball bats to storefront windows, steal cars, and do drugs...do you really think you're stronger than all the other people who've gone before you? Surely you know that adage comes from the Bible, and God gave us that command for a reason?"

"I don't think I'm stronger, Daddy, I just think I can't abandon someone who calls me their friend, just because they've done things that I don't agree with."

His lips flattened, even as he nodded and then looked away. At the orange walls and the doorway that led into the living room, where their old comfortable furniture sat grouped so that he could lie on the couch and the girls could each sit in a recliner and they could chat while he did a little extra work on the day job and they did their schoolwork.

It could be one of his girls in jail right now.

His heart clenched and hurt at the thought while his mind rebelled. No. Not his daughters.

"I don't ever want to have to bail either one of you out of jail."

"I don't want to ever embarrass you like that, Dad. I don't want to hurt the town and the people who love me and treat me like I'm a part of them," Naomi said, slowly, as though she were feeling her way.

His eyes slipped to Lexi, who was watching their conversation, but as was typical with Lexi, she was processing everything and not really talking.

He looked back at Naomi. "What about your sister? What about the influence Macy might have on her?"

"I'm not saying Lexi has to, I'm just saying, asking, that you not tell me I can't stand beside my friend."

"Maybe she'll stop," Lexi said, her words much less emotional than Naomi's. "I don't want to do a bunch of things that are going to get me in trouble. If that's what Macy's going to do, I'll just stay here and practice my flute. Maybe I'll get more hours at the ice-cream shop if it opens back up," she said, her voice falling a little on that last part, like she'd remembered that maybe she wouldn't have a job.

"Can I think about that, Naomi?" he said finally. He'd never faced anything like this in his parenting before.

Naomi nodded slowly.

And then, suddenly everything came into sharp focus.

"You know what? Never mind. I trust you, and I know you want the best for your friend, and I know you mean it when you say that you're not interested in doing the things that she does." He tapped his two index fingers together, lifting his head. "I do think you need to remember, though, we have a tendency to be like our friends, so if Macy's going to continue to hang out with the people she did this with, I think you'd be wise to step back. But you're almost eighteen. It's not going to be too long, and you're going to need to be making these decisions for yourself. You can make this one. I'm not gonna forbid you to see anyone. I'm not going to forbid you to hang out with anyone. Because I trust you, because I believe that you're going to do right."

Maybe he was making the worst decision of his fatherhood career, but the rightness of it settled down deep, and he felt like trusting his daughter, and letting her know that he trusted her, was the best thing that he could do.

Maybe she'd mess up. People did. But him being a helicopter parent, not allowing her to breathe or to make the decision that she felt was right, that aligned with the beliefs and values that he'd been teaching her all her life, wasn't the right decision. He was sure of it.

Of course, he hadn't been planning on not spending time with Zoriah because of her niece. His daughters might have pointed out that flaw in the logic if he hadn't let them hang out with Macy anymore, but he still saw Zoriah.

Though, she hadn't answered the text he'd sent her last night, and she hadn't answered his phone call this morning.

Maybe she was going to cut him off.

That would be irony.

"I don't know how to get into the jail, but I'd like to visit if I can," Naomi said, taking a small spoonful of her oatmeal, lifting it up, then putting it back down. Unless he had totally missed it, she hadn't eaten a single bite.

"I think it'd be really nice of you. I think Macy would appreciate it," he said. "Let me talk to Miss Zoriah, and maybe we can all go together. Or maybe she'd rather we stagger our visits," he added, just in case Zoriah insisted that she didn't want to be anywhere near them. "If you guys are okay, I think I'll walk across the street and see if I can talk to her."

"Why don't you just call her?" Lexi said, scraping the last of her oatmeal from her bowl.

"I think I'd rather see her," he said, not bothering to admit that she hadn't answered his call. There was no need. His girls didn't need to know everything.

"I think Naomi is right, and I'd like to go to the jail too," Lexi said, her lips a little twisted but her look thoughtful.

"Of course. I'd love it if you'd both go."

He pushed back from the table, knowing that the next hour or so could determine whether or not he had a future with Zoriah.

Chapter 20

Zoriah lay face down on the floor, the carpet rough against her cheek.

It had been late by the time Mark had gone to sleep, and he wasn't up yet.

Zoriah had never fallen asleep at all. She'd finally gotten out of bed and lay on her face beside it, her heart too heavy and sore and broken to be able to find words to pray, but she supposed God knew exactly what she wanted to say.

God understood her pain, her deep sorrow and her longing for her niece, even if she couldn't get it into words. He saw her tears, felt her broken heart.

She heard someone knocking on the apartment door, and hoped they would go away, turning her head toward the wall like that would make it stop.

Had she not locked her shop?

Gage had a key. He'd been there through everything from the beginning and had helped her with so much. She'd given him a key so he could let himself in and out rather than having to text her.

Because she trusted him.

Just like she trusted Macy.

The thought hurt.

What could she have done differently? Maybe if she hadn't been so set on getting the store open...maybe if she had stayed in Ohio and continued to work at her job, she would have had more time to pay attention and maybe she would have noticed the signs.

How could she have missed them? Surely there were signs. There had to have been.

Her sister would have been so disappointed in her. Zoriah felt like she let her down. She'd promised her sister she'd take care of her children and look at what she had allowed to happen.

She ignored the knocking again, wanting to shout, "Go away!" but she didn't.

Hopefully whoever it was, whether it was Gage or someone he'd given a key to, would leave. She could see Iva May coming to visit. Or Lindy. Or any of the ladies in town.

They'd been too nice to her. Zoriah wanted them to be unkind to her. She wanted to suffer. She deserved to suffer.

She didn't want to think about her friends and neighbors who had accepted her without question, encouraged her and helped her. She couldn't think about Gage either.

She just couldn't.

She didn't deserve to have someone like him. Surely God would see that now and take him away.

Her brain registered there were footsteps coming up the stairs, just before the door opened and Gage's voice spoke almost tentatively, "Zoriah? Are you up?"

The floor creaked more, and then the door closed.

She supposed it was too much to hope that he had turned around, gone back down and shut the door behind him.

Sure enough, footsteps came again, crossing the kitchen floor.

"Zoriah?"

He wouldn't come back to her bedroom. She was sure of it, so she lay on the floor, barely breathing, and waited for him to leave.

"Zoriah? Are you in here?"

What felt like long years later, she heard movement, but she didn't allow herself a sigh of relief, and wouldn't, not until she heard the door close behind him and his footsteps going back down the stairs.

"Zoriah? Are you okay?"

The voice was closer. It sounded like he was standing at her bedroom door, and then the air moved, and he was kneeling beside her with his hand on her back.

He must want to cut ties with her immediately for him to walk into her home and bedroom without an invitation.

She held herself still as she lay on her stomach on the floor, her faced pressed into the carpet. She didn't want to deal with this now. Couldn't. She needed time to come to terms with the flip flop turn her life had taken.

"Hey. I see you breathing." He seemed to pause as though he were trying to figure out what to say. She shook her head, wanting to head him off.

"No. You don't have to say anything. I understand," she said, her voice sounding like she was crying, but she couldn't help it, because she was. She couldn't stop the tears.

Tears because her niece was in jail, and there was nothing she could do about it. No way she could protect her. She knew, even as she wanted to go and break her out, that that was where her niece needed to be. She needed to face the consequences of her actions. As much as Zoriah wanted to shelter her and shield her from them.

Her heart broke, and she couldn't shake the guilt and shame.

"You understand?" Gage said, sounding baffled.

"I do. It's fine. I know your girls can't be around Macy anymore, and I know that you and I can't be together because of that. I get it. You can go, and there are no hard feelings."

She meant that. She really didn't have hard feelings. That had been going through her mind all night too. Macy was at the forefront, but she cared about Gage. Far more than she wanted to admit.

If her heart hadn't already been broken, it would have been crushed at the thought of letting Gage go.

Maybe that accounted for the almost unmanageable pain, physical pain, in her chest.

"Who said that?" he asked in that same tone that totally lacked comprehension.

His hand moved over her back and rested between her shoulder blades, moving so softly and so sweetly, it would have brought tears to her eyes if they hadn't already been flooded.

"I just know it. I told you I understand and it's okay." She had to quit crying. She had to pull herself together and act like an adult.

"Are you sick?"

She shook her head. Why would he ask that?

"Why are you lying face down on the floor? You scared me to death when I saw you like this."

"Praying." She wanted to apologize for scaring him, wanted to tell him not to worry about her, wanted to say that she would be fine, but she'd barely been able to quit crying all night, and right now it would seem like a total lie.

It would be true. Eventually.

She would get through this, just like she'd gotten through everything else in her life. Losing her parents, losing her grandmother, her sister's illness and then her death, moving with her niece and nephew and opening her grandmother's store. God had held her hand through it all.

Although each time He'd given her someone to lean on.

She was down to Mark and while he seemed to be doing okay, she needed to be strong for him, not expect him to hold her hand.

"Do you want me to leave you alone with your prayers?" Gage asked, sounding reluctant, almost like he didn't want to leave, although she knew he did.

"That's for the best. A clean, fast break hurts less in the long run."

She didn't think he was so stuck on her that this would be a problem for him. She was pretty sure she was much more fond of him than he was of her. How could she not be after all the help that he'd given her?

"I... I didn't tell my girls they couldn't see Macy. In fact, they want to go visit her at the jail later today. I didn't know if we could all go together?"

Her eyes opened wide, her lashes brushing against the carpet.

"Can I talk to you for a couple of minutes?" he asked, hesitantly.

"Yeah?"

"Would you look at me?"

She didn't want to. Her face would be tear-streaked and there were probably big bags under her eyes from not sleeping all night. Maybe that was part of the reason she couldn't stop crying, because she was so tired. But she couldn't get her brain to rest or sleep.

Without answering him, she pushed up, sad and a little bereft when his hand fell off her back, as she gathered her legs under her and looked at him.

"Sorry about the mess," she said pointing to her face.

"You didn't answer my text," he said, ignoring or not noticing her face.

Although his words didn't sound like an accusation, they almost felt like it, because of the hurt in his voice.

"I told you. A clean break is easier."

"So you're breaking up with me?" His words were slow.

"No. You're breaking with me. It's fine. I told you I understand."

"And I told you that wasn't right. I'm not. So, if you're not that means we're not breaking up." His brows were still drawn down, like he wasn't sure whether she was going to agree with him or not.

"You can't be with me. Your girls. Macy. The town. I don't even know if I can stay here!"

"You can. This isn't you. This is your niece. And we'll handle it together. The town isn't going to shun you because your niece screwed up."

"They should. It's all my fault."

"It is not."

"If I hadn't been so wrapped up in opening the store, maybe I would have noticed what was going on with her."

"You're a great step-in mom. You pay attention to her. This is the kind of thing that anyone could miss. Especially since Macy's been through so much. I know you've been doing the best you can. The rest of the town knows it too. We've seen you and we admire how you've taken your sister's children and done your very best with them."

She had trouble believing his words, but they were soothing to her soul in a way that she desperately needed. She hadn't realized how she'd longed for that comfort. How the lies that she'd been telling herself had been so hurtful.

"Is that really true?"

"Of course it is."

"You don't hate me?" she asked. She needed the confirmation.

"Of course not. In fact... I realized last night, or maybe, I've known it for a while...that I'm...falling in love with you."

His hand landed gently on her knee, and he seemed to search her eyes.

"I guess this isn't the best timing, but I was scared when you didn't answer my text. I thought you were going to walk away from me, from us. I've had some of the best times of my life just hanging out with you and working together in your shop. I want to spend *more* time with you, not less."

"I don't know what's going to happen. I don't know what I'm going to have to do." Zoriah managed to keep her eyes from filling again.

It was also confusing. Hopefully Macy would be able to get out of jail but surely they were going to charge her, there would be a trial, which meant lawyers and probably jail time and the thoughts were overwhelming, so over-whelming she could hardly think.

"Let's just take it a day at a time. I don't know what's going to happen, either. There will be a lot of different decisions that people have to make, and Macy will have to face the consequences of what she's done, but she can face those consequences with you and I beside her. I'm not fighting any of the judgement that needs handed out, but supporting her as she pays the penalty for her crimes."

Zoriah nodded. That was exactly how she felt. They couldn't fight any charges, or any punishments. Macy deserved them.

"You're right, but I don't want you to feel like you have to. I don't want you to think that this is what you have to do. I don't want you to feel you have to be with me if you don't want to be."

"Trust me. I'm here because this is exactly where I want to be." He took a deep breath. "I'm here because...I love you."

Her mouth dropped. He was serious. He'd said it before, but his words hadn't been registering, she'd been so distressed. So sure that he was coming here to say something completely different, she hadn't truly heard him, now she realized he'd said it, and she'd completely ignored him.

"I don't deserve that."

"I think you do. Regardless, I think a lot of times we get things we don't deserve. But it doesn't matter. I love you. Nothing you can do is going to change that. Even if you send me away, it's not going to make me stop loving you."

"I was listening but I wasn't really hearing you. I thought that you were going to tell me you wanted to break up with me, that your kids weren't going to be allowed to be around Macy anymore, which I understand - "

"No," he interrupted her. "Naomi pretty much begged me to allow her to stand beside Macy. She's not going to hang out with Macy if Macy continues to be close to the people who influenced her to do this, but for now, Naomi wants to support her and be a true friend to her. That's the right decision. And that's what I want to do for you." He said the last with a little softer, slightly lower pitch, and his words touched Zoriah's heart.

"I can't believe it."

"You need to, because it's true."

She gulped air. "I love you too. That's part of why I was crying. Part of why I was praying. Because I thought this would destroy whatever we had, and I was going to have to let you go."

"I'm not going anywhere. I want to stay beside you."

"I don't deserve that, but thank you," she said, wishing there were words for her to say more, but unable to think of anything. Words didn't begin to cover what was in her heart, the gratitude and the relief and the comfort in knowing that she was not alone, that not only had God heard her prayer, but he'd sent someone to stand beside her through this trial.

"You probably haven't eaten anything since last night."

"I haven't been hungry."

"How about we get up, see if we can find something? I heard Mark stirring in the other room and both of you should eat a little, even if you're not hungry. Maybe we can cook it together?"

Her lips tilted. She determined she would eat if it would make him happy, not only because he was right, but because she appreciated him making the effort to take care of her.

He started to move, but she stopped him, putting her hand over his, linking their fingers together.

"Thank you. Thank you so much for coming, but more than that, thank you for not leaving me when I needed you, even though people, including me, would understand and even expect you to. I appreciate it."

"You can thank me if you want to, but I'm just doing what I want to do, which is to be with you. Whatever you're going through, I want to share with you." He squeezed her fingers. "Isn't that what love is? Good times and bad?"

She nodded slowly. "I guess."

"You're not leaving your niece, right? Not just because you feel like you owe your sister, but because you love Macy. That's what love does. It sticks. No matter what."

"She's going to need me to show her that, because, she probably will have as hard of a time believing that anyone could actually love her like that as I do."

"Then we'll show her."

"You too?"

"I'm with you. Whatever that means."

She didn't know what she'd done to deserve him, but she leaned toward him, taking her free hand and putting it around his shoulders, pressing her face into his neck.

"Thank you."

"Thank you. You could have told me to leave. Thank you for letting me stay."

He held her for a bit. She had to admit it felt good to be able to lean on someone.

Mark eventually came to the door, and they all went out to the table and got breakfast ready together, talking to Mark about Macy, and answering his questions as best they could.

He claimed to have no idea that Macy had been hanging out with the wrong crowd, and Zoriah believed him. He'd been moved around just as much as his sister and he'd been focused on making friends and trying to fit into a new place and school and getting over the death of his mother.

She supposed none of them had been thinking very clearly.

Chapter 29

At 1:30 Gage and his girls, along with Zoriah and Mark, left for the jail. If Zoriah thought that she would find Macy in tears, contrite and cowed, she was disappointed.

Macy stood behind bars, unemotional, and cold.

She resisted the overtures of her friends, and barely spoke.

Zoriah wanted to rail at her, ask her what she'd been doing when she destroyed everyone's property, and now she was acting so unrepentant and almost arrogant.

Although Macy wasn't smiling, just the fact that she didn't seem to feel bad, stirred anger that Zoriah had trouble controlling.

Up until that point she'd been hurt and sad and even scared, along with guilty and sure everything was all her fault, but now, anger took over. It was all she could do not to storm out of the jail, or grab a hold of her niece and shake her until she started to feel remorse and make sense.

When they arrived home, the police had finished gathering evidence and the town was quiet. The streets had been swept and the windows boarded up, but Blueberry Beach still reminded her more of a war zone than of the town she loved.

Naomi, who was not her normal happy self, along with Lexi and Mark, who had borrowed Gage's skates, skated on the road along with Mark's friend and Sierra while Gage and Zoriah sat on camp chairs on the sidewalk.

Anger had been simmering in Zoriah since they'd left the jail. It had gotten even sharper and stronger during the afternoon as she visited with her neighbors and friends and watched them try to pick up the pieces and clean up the wreckage of their lives and businesses.

"You want to talk about it?" Gage asked, her hand securely tucked in his and sitting on the arm of his chair.

"I'm not sure I can. I've run the gauntlet of emotions, I guess. Shock, shame, guilt, and now this overwhelming anger that makes me want to just strangle her. How could she act like that?"

"Maybe she was hiding her true feelings?"

Zoriah's head snapped around to him. "Today? In the jail?"

He nodded.

"Why would she hide the feelings she knows she should be showing? And show us something she knows is wrong?"

"Because guilt, sadness, being contrite and apologies... They're weak. They show weakness. Vulnerability. And maybe, she's afraid she's going to be rejected, so she has to cover it with emotions that seem to say strength."

Zoriah knew her mouth hung open, as she stared at Gage, not really seeing him but processing his words.

"How did you get to be so astute?" She finally asked, because his words had rung true to her. If she were afraid, especially if she knew she were wrong and didn't want to admit it, or wanted to admit it but didn't know how everyone would react to her, didn't have a mother's loving arms to cling to, she might hide it with those emotions. With emotions she knew wouldn't hurt her and wouldn't leave her open to rejection.

"I have girls, remember?"

"Really?" She gave him a look that said she figured he was naturally caring and it didn't have much at all to do with his girls.

He laughed. Not a full deep-throated laugh, the kind they'd shared last night, but one that was more subdued, acknowledging all the things that had transpired in the last twenty-four hours, but still saying that they could share happiness. That joy wasn't gone forever, just hidden behind a cloud for a while.

"No. I guess I've thought more about those things than I would have if I hadn't had girls, though. Sometimes I wonder if my marriage might have survived if I'd been a little smarter back then."

"You think it would have?" she asked, maybe not sure she wanted to know the answer. She couldn't be jealous of someone who was long gone and never coming back. He didn't harbor tender feelings for his ex, nor secretly long to be back with her. At least, Zoriah was fairly certain he didn't. As though he noticed her insecurity, his fingers tightened around hers, and his other hand came over and tucked her hand against his side.

"No. I don't think she's the kind of woman who cares about any vows she makes. I think, no matter how understanding and sensitive I would have been, she wasn't interested in staying married, not because of me, but because of her."

"I guess I just can't imagine her not appreciating what she had."

He gave her a flat look. "I'm not anything to brag about. But two imperfect people can stay together if they're both determine to make it work. One determined person isn't enough. And she wasn't committed. In fact I think she was bored and wanted out, felt tied down with the girls, craved the excitement of someone new."

Zoriah nodded. She understood. That was probably typical. Falling in love was the fun part. Staying together took work and sacrifice. Things most people didn't want to give.

"Regardless, as I watched Macy in her cell today, I thought she might be hiding her true feelings of remorse behind that hard, indifferent wall."

"I have anger, but it is mostly because of what she had done to the friends and neighbors who had been so good to us. I wasn't really thinking about her. But now that I've been gone for a couple of hours, and had a chance to think about it, I am struck by what you'd said to me when you were in my bedroom this morning about love."

"Really? What was that?"

The kids skated by, still not laughing and as carefree as usual, but having fun nonetheless, their chatter drifting on the breeze and making the town, despite the boarded windows and dark storefronts, feel cozy and homey.

"I've told Macy over and over again how much I love her. If I get angry at her, blow up at her and come unglued on her because of what she's done, I'm not really showing love, am I?"

"Actions have consequences."

"I agree. But the consequences don't have to be delivered in anger. They should be delivered in love, right?"

Gage nodded thoughtfully, then one side of his lip tugged up. "I think you've become a philosopher."

"You had that effect on me. Because it's what you said that got me thinking."

"That's kind of scary. Every once in a while something intelligent comes out of my mouth, but most the time it's just gibberish. Don't take it to heart."

"Actually, that's one of the things that attracted me to you. I think the first day we met you were telling me things that I'd never thought about before. Your words made me think. You didn't even know it. But I had to reconsider the things I knew. Or at least thought to be true. I can't say I necessarily changed my mind about anything, but, I've definitely changed the way I think. I like that you challenge me."

"I like that you don't get offended by my ideas," he said. "Although I still think you're giving me more credit than I deserve."

"No. Definitely not."

"So what are you going to do? There should be some repercussions, right?" he asked.

"I don't know. I'll pray about it. I have until Monday. At the jail, the trooper said we could come back and see her tomorrow afternoon. Maybe things will change."

She hoped so. It would be so much easier to deal with a child who was contrite and sorry for what she'd done, than one who didn't seem to care.

"Whatever you want me to do, if you want me with you while you talk to her, if you don't, just tell me. I want to help you however I can," Gage said, as his hand stroked over her fingers.

"Thank you," she said, on a little puff of air. "That seems like all I ever say to you anymore."

She meant it. She supposed, if Gage would stay with her through this, through the embarrassment of having a child arrested, through the concern of his daughters being influenced by her, through the chance that their neighbors and friends would think he was crazy for staying, she supposed, she could trust him to stay with her through anything.

"I've never been with a man who loved me more than he loved his reputation, or the things that he did, or...more than anything aside from his children." She couldn't think of anything Gage put ahead of her.

It was humbling.

Just then his phone buzzed, and he pulled it out of his pocket, looking at it. It took her about two seconds to figure out it was terrible news, since he stiffened beside her, and seemed to freeze, his lungs stopping, and his face bent down.

"What?"

"It's my boss. He said he wanted to give me a warning, that on Monday everyone would be getting pink slips. Proverbial ones, since I probably won't get an actual physical one."

"You lost your job. Oh no."

It never rains but it pours.

The proverb that she'd grown up hearing from her mom and her grandma trotted through her head.

She wanted to ask what he was going to do, but she assumed he probably didn't know.

"What can I do?"

He shook his head. "It's not a catastrophe. I have money put aside. I'd hoped to help pay for the girls' college with it, but I can use it to live on."

"That's good," she said, but she sensed he wasn't done.

"And of course, I'll look for another job. It'd be great to find something that I could do from home, but...that might not be possible."

And then it hit her. He might be moving. He might have to leave Blueberry Beach. If he couldn't find something that he could do remotely, he might have to go closer to Chicago, or at least a suburb. Or possibly west to Ann Arbor, or even Detroit.

Somewhere where he could do something to support his family.

Her stomach felt like it had fallen to her toes. She thought she'd cried every tear she could possibly cry, but the idea that he might be leaving made her want to curl up in a ball or at least wrap her arms around her stomach and bend over. Groaning.

"I don't want you to go," she said, and she couldn't stop the quiver in her voice. Normally she felt like she was so much stronger than this, but surely she'd had enough, had been given enough.

"I don't want to go. I'll try hard not to."

"I know. I'm sorry. I'm…I feel like I should handle this better, but it just feels like more than I can take right now. You've been such a rock."

News like that was why she hated to be dependent on anyone, because it seemed like everyone always left.

His presence beside her, strong and solid, steadied her.

His voice was calm, reassuring. "If I weren't here, Iva May would be over here sitting beside you right now. Lindy, Anitra, even Beverly would be here. Bill would be standing there ready to do whatever you asked him to, and I even heard that Mr. Shoemaker's granddaughter is coming back."

"Laura?" she asked, excited that the quiet man who owned the miniature doll store at the other end of the street might be welcoming her old friend back.

"Is that her name? I'm not sure."

"That's the only granddaughter I know." Mr. Shoemaker made miniature towns by hand, carving them and painting them himself.

His shop had not been vandalized other than the door being broken, probably since it sat at the edge of town and didn't have any large glass show windows.

"The ladies at the diner said you and she used to be friends."

"We did. But, I guess like a lot of people, we lost touch over the years." She'd love to see Laura again, and she also knew that Gage was right. Her neighbors and her friends and her fellow business owners would support her however she needed.

"But I guess you know that's not the same as having you," she said, her eyes going to his, and her brows raised.

"Thank you. I think that was a compliment."

"It was."

The kids had been skating on the street, more subdued than usual, although occasionally their conversation and laughter drifted over, making it feel like a summer night from her childhood.

Different, since neither her grandma nor her sister were there, and it was hard to forget her niece was in jail and hard not to be wishing with all her heart every second that she could do something about that. But the night air was sweet, the breeze off the lake fresh and clean and pure and the man beside her true.

"This is a beautiful moment." Her words merged with the fresh lake air, soft and quiet, intimate, and he turned to look at her as she continued, "I guess the best thing to do with your life is enjoy each day, each moment, and not let the things that are bothering you, the things you wish you could change, the things you worry about…not let any of that ruin these beautiful moments that make up your life."

"The beautiful forevers. You'll look back on this day, on this evening, on us," he held up the hands that were clasped between them. "And it will be a beautiful memory, forever."

She smiled, and they sat in silence for a while.

She didn't know how late it was when she finally stretched and stood and said, "It's late. I'd better make sure Mark gets to bed. I don't think anybody slept very well last night."

"I agree." He stood beside her, not letting go of her hand, but pulling her closer. "Are you going to be okay?"

"I am. I have the Lord to lean on tonight, and He gave me you. What more could a girl want?"

"Seems like you didn't get a very good deal with that last thing," he said. "And I'm not digging for compliments."

"I did think of one more thing I wouldn't mind having."

"Yeah?" he asked, sounding eager that he might be able to help her with something.

"A good night kiss might be nice," she whispered.

"I thought you'd never ask me," he said, his lips curving up.

She laughed as his head lowered and his arms wrapped around her and she leaned into him and his lips touched hers and her fingers curled around the back of his neck and her heart grew big and wide with all the love she felt for him, racing, and thumping against her chest and the night got infinitely sweeter and more beautiful.

She could hear the kids calling each other at the far end of the street when Gage finally lifted his head.

"I'm not sure that was a good night kiss, or an I-want-more kiss," he said, sounding a little out of breath.

"It was an I-want-more kiss," she said, having the same out of breath problem that he did.

"I think it was a I-don't-know-what-kind-of-job-I'm-going-to-get-but-I-can't-leave-you kiss," he said, and his words might have upset her, reminding her of his uncertain future, but his smile was a little carefree, like his job didn't matter as much as she did, and she smiled back, suddenly feeling like everything was going to work out.

Maybe not right away, maybe not the way she wanted it to, but in some way that would be perfect. And completely good for everyone.

"I agree. That's definitely the kind of kiss it was."

"Let's go for the good night kiss now," he said, and lowered his head again.

Chapter 22

Macy

I'm standing in my room, at the window, looking out towards Lake Michigan.

I can't see it, of course. Not only is it dark out, but the dunes are too high and there's a shed between Grandma Heater's building and the end of town anyway.

Not that it matters.

My life is over.

I've screwed up too badly to fix.

I knew it was dangerous to live the double life that I had fallen into.

My mom had no idea. And yeah, it goes back at least that far, even further.

I don't know why.

School was easy for me. I got good grades. I was in the honor society, and president of the Young Christians club. Not to mention I was on student council, as well as head of the youth group at our church, a choir member, band member, head of the debate team, and the secretary of the parliamentary procedure team.

I was in everything. The perfect student.

I also played volleyball, ran track, and was just a thousand points away from being the highest scoring girls basketball player our school had ever seen.

Until we moved, of course.

The move didn't really bother me. I make friends easily, and I wasn't worried about it. There were a few things I wouldn't be able to achieve because I had to change schools, and I had to make new friends, but it wasn't that hard.

I might have even left the double life behind.

While I was all of those other things, I was also running around with the wrong crowd on weekends. We just did stupid stuff, like race cars, play chicken, and smoke joints.

We did a little shoplifting at the mall, which I didn't even really need to do because it wasn't like I needed anything.

It was just for the thrill. I don't even know why. Something to do to get my mind off everything that was wrong at home? My dad not wanting me. My mom sick and dying and me not being able to control any of it?

Regardless, my mom didn't have a clue, and of course Aunt Zoriah is as clueless as anyone has ever been.

I could tell she was overwhelmed with my brother and I. She means well, but she falls for every trick in the book and believed that I was the goody-goody I pretended to be and I pretty much get away with whatever I want.

I never thought I'd get caught. Maybe no one ever does. I'd never stolen a car before. And I'd never damaged property. Those things are new.

Regardless, I know Aunt Zoriah's gonna come down on me like a ton of bricks. I've already been kicked off of everything I can be kicked off of. I can't do anything at school except sit in the classroom and come straight home.

I haven't talked to them, but I'm sure Mr. Adam and Miss Lindy won't have anything to do with me, so I can kiss my job at the candy store goodbye.

I'm sure Aunt Zoriah isn't going to let me work at her store. Not now that she knows I steal stuff.

It wouldn't surprise me if she sent me to foster care, or whatever they do with kids like me. Kids they can't trust.

She hasn't said anything to me since she posted my bail. I've gone to school for a week and all I heard from Aunt Zoriah was that she was thinking and would talk to me when she was ready. It's Friday night and she said this evening at supper that she's ready. I'm waiting.

I know she's pretty much going to tie me to my bed post, and I deserve it.

I deserve whatever punishment she's gonna level on me. I'm a terrible person.

The townspeople had rallied together and come to her aid, *our* aid, and made sure that we had whatever we needed in order to start up the business in Gram's old shop and be successful. The townspeople had done so much for us, and I'd betrayed everyone.

Whatever Aunt Zoriah does to me, I deserve that and a whole lot worse.

I wish I could go back and change it. I wish I could fix it somehow. I see now what a thin line I was walking, but I've always gotten away with anything bad I've done, so the consequences weren't real.

I guess I probably deserve to be in jail. The idea scares me some, but the idea of facing felony charges, and maybe going to adult prison, will I have to fight? Will people hurt me?

I'm scared. I've never been this scared in my life before. And I can't let anyone know it. If I allow one crack in my armor, I will crumble.

I wish I had my mom.

I just want my mom to come in, put her arms around me, and hold me close. I want to smell her elegant perfumed scent, and have her run her hand over my hair and call me her Marvelous Macy and tell me that we'd make a Starbucks run, and I would get my very own coffee. That was our special treat.

I know I don't deserve that, or anything else good.

I have my hands crossed over my chest. And although the sound of the door opening startles me, I don't move from my position.

I deserve what I'm going to get. I know she hates me, and she has every right to. Everyone hates me. I hate that thought, but I'm not going to grovel, and I'm not going to show weakness. Life has already tried to beat me down. I don't have a dad, he doesn't want me, doesn't love me enough to stay, then my mom gets sick, then she dies and then I move across the country.

I'll probably wake up tomorrow morning with cancer.

Regardless, I hear footsteps, and then the door closes.

I'm waiting for the yelling to start. She deserves to be able to yell at me. And I'll let her.

"Macy?"

I wasn't expecting that tone. It's not timid but it's not angry either. It almost sounds like she's hurt.

I want the anger. I can handle the anger. If she's hurt, if she cries, I'm going to fall apart too.

I turn toward her, and she looks sad but determined. I keep my arms held tight across my chest. I'm ready.

My eyes drop, and I notice she's holding a book with her finger stuck in it, keeping her place.

Great. In addition to being yelled at, she's going to give me a lecture from the Bible. Maybe when she's done, she'll hit me over the head with it.

Nothing better to spread hate to somebody than to tell them how miserably they've failed and then hit them over the head with religion.

I want to run. But I narrow my eyes and wait.

"It's been a hard few days, hasn't it?" Aunt Zoriah says.

My lips flatten. I knot my brows.

"I guess," I say, although I want to say that's a major understatement. I don't know why she starting out being nice to me. I know I'm getting it. I wish she'd just get it over with.

"I wanted to read this to you if you don't mind," she says, and I look at her shoulder. She might as well get started telling me how I don't measure up.

She opens the book, the pages crinkling. I swallow, and it sounds like a gunshot in my quiet room.

The sound of the pages crinkling is reminiscent of my mom reading to us when we were little. I loved that time, when we snuggled in bed with her, warm against her side, me on one side, and Mark on the other. She'd read to us from the Bible first.

Once in a while she'd talk about what she read, and then she might get a storybook out or a longer book with or without pictures. I didn't care. I like looking at the pictures, but just being able to snuggle up with my mom was treat enough. And then she'd start to read and she'd take us to somewhere far away, stories about kids who had two parents, or kids who were brave, or men who acted with valor and courage. A lot of stories, and they inspired me to want to do more with my life.

Funny how the things we want as kids are usually not the way we end up being.

Aunt Zoriah clears her throat and then she begins to read: "For I am persuaded that neither death, nor life, nor angels, nor principalities, nor powers, nor things present, nor things to come, nor height, nor depth, nor any other creature, shall be able to separate us from the love of God, which is in Christ Jesus our Lord."

Aunt Zoriah closes the book.

I know a lot of passages from the Bible, a lot of ones that she could apply to my situation starting with the Ten Commandments and going all through the New Testament.

This wasn't the passage I expected.

She clears her throat. "I just want you to know, whatever happens, whatever you do, no matter what, I love you now, and I will love you always."

My throat tightens, my stomach feels flat like a pancake and my chest feels empty. I struggle to breathe.

"I don't think I need to punish you. I think you know what you did was wrong, and I think you're facing enough. I just wanted you know, I'm not going to try to get you out of any punishment that you've earned for yourself, but I will be right there beside you as much as I can, with you through everything. Because I love you. And nothing will change that."

I blow out a breath, trying to keep my façade up.

What she said has alleviated my biggest fear. I'm scared to death to face this alone. It was one thing to break into the stores, break the windows, steal, but it was always with my friends beside me. Now they're nowhere to be found, and I'm here by myself. I'll be standing in court by myself. Except...it looks like Aunt Zoriah will be with me.

"Do you mean that?" I can't help but ask. It seems...unbelievable to me.

"I do. I love you."

"Aren't you...going to yell at me?" I asked, uncertainly.

This feels weird. I was expecting screaming and punishment and a lecture about how I've embarrassed her and let her down and how I've brought shame on the family by my behavior and how Grandma Heater would be disappointed in me and how mom would be rolling over in her grave and all of those things that adults say whenever they're angry, and yet...she gave me grace instead.

"No. The most important thing is that I love you no matter what. Nothing else matters," she says, although I hear sadness and disappointment in her tone — or maybe it's my imagination.

She smiles a little bit at me, and I can't stand here with my arms crossed any longer if I tried.

My face crumbles, the tears I've been shoving back for days now finally break loose, and I take three big steps, throwing myself into her arms.

I'm a teenager and too big for this, but I put my head on her chest and I burrow under her chin and I sob, big ugly sobs that feel like they've been ripped from someplace deep inside of me, tearing off like Velcro, and making my throat raw. My sobs break the silence of the room as my tears pour down.

Her hand rubs over my hair like my mom's used to, and she murmurs about nothing and everything, comforting and sweet.

I don't know how long we stand there, her arms around me, holding me like my mom, while the remorse has settled like a lead cape over the top of me, and I press into her harder.

I've done something terrible. Not necessarily the vandalism, and the thievery. That can be paid for.

I've embarrassed my family. I've taken advantage of people's trust. I've been terrible to our neighbors who have been kind to me and my family, who helped us when we needed it. Instead of paying them back with kindness, I paid them back with betrayal, and nastiness.

My mom would be so disappointed in me. Is this how I want to represent her now that she's gone?

Finally, I pull back far enough to say, still sobbing, "I hate myself. I wish I were dead!"

Maybe someday I'll look back on that and say it was teenage drama, but right now, I mean it with all my heart.

I'm vile and despicable and I detest what I have become. What I've allowed myself to be when I know no adults are watching.

"Someone loved you enough to die for you," Aunt Zoriah says very softly, and also calmly. "Regardless of whether you hate yourself or not, the very least you can do, is live for Him."

I represent my mom. I also represent Someone else, and I've let Him down, too.

"How can I do that now? I've destroyed everything!"

"Wherever you are, whatever you do, whether you're in a palace or you're in prison, every breath you take can be for Him."

"People will laugh at me now. I was a fake for so long."

"It doesn't matter. God judges the heart. He knows whether you're sincere. And you know no one else can judge your heart and know whether you mean what you say or not."

Boy was she right. I'd fooled too many people for so long. I just wish I had the chance to go back and apologize, to my mom, especially.

And right there, that's what does it for me.

The undeserved grace that Aunt Zoriah has shown me has given me a concrete example of what Jesus did for me.

Up until this point in my life, I'd heard all about grace and love and the sacrifice of Christ, but it wasn't real until this moment, when I see it clearly in action.

It is real to me now in a way it never has been before.

That knowledge sinks down deep while I struggle with the more immediate thought of what I'm going to do.

The idea that I don't want to live my life with regrets, wishing I can apologize to people who've passed on, I don't ever want to have that feeling again.

The way to do that, I see clearly, is to start right now, living the kind of life I know I should. The kind of life that puts Jesus and others ahead of myself. If I do that I know I will never again act in a way that will bring shame and embarrassment on me or my family.

I swallow hard because I know what I need to do. I know what I was expecting to have to be forced to do, and now, no one will have to force me. I want to.

Even if I'm afraid.

"I need to go to Mr. Bill and Mr. Ethan and to John and Anitra and to Adam and Lindy and I need to apologize to them." I close my eyes. My breathing is faster just thinking of their reactions. I'm scared, but if I'm going to change, no, if I'm going to allow Jesus to change me, this is a big first step.

"Tomorrow. We can do it tomorrow whenever you want." Aunt Zoriah says, rubbing her hand on my back. "Are you okay?" She leans back and looks deep into my eyes.

I nod, so tempted to ask her to tuck me in and sit with me and hold my hand. Scared to death to face the night alone. Scared to face any of the future. While I know she said she'd stand with me and everything I had to face, I can't get to heaven on Aunt Zoriah's coattails. I need to talk to the Lord, and I need to do it by myself.

"I'm okay, thank you. Thank you for giving me what I didn't deserve."

Her lips turn up, and a sad, small smile, one that acknowledges all of the difficulty still ahead for us, but one that also acknowledges that she believes me. Even though she knew that I'd been living a lie for a really long time, she believes me and trusts me. That means almost as much to me as the fact that she still loves me.

"Good night Aunt Zoriah," I say.

"Good night, Macy."

Chapter 23

"The sentencing wasn't bad," Gage said, as he held Zoriah's hand, walking along the beach of Lake Michigan. It was well after dark, although there were still tourists strolling along slowly as they were doing.

"No. Macy can thank her neighbors, and God, and a judge who believed her, for that," Zoriah said, sounding relieved and happy and thankful.

"Do you think she'll be able to spend the summer on house arrest?" Gage asked, feeling like she could, but Zoriah hadn't given her opinion, and he was curious how she felt about it. It was an unusual sentence for a teenager.

"Yes. She was determined to do whatever it took. In the two months that she's been out, she's helped everyone on the street repair their businesses, and in fact I've actually had to tell her to slow down and take it easy, because she's been driving herself so hard."

"Is that bad?" he asked, thinking that maybe Macy thought somehow she could atone for sin by her own efforts, and while that would make it up to people, it wasn't what the Lord wanted.

"I think it's good. She and I talked about it when I've asked her to slow down. I reminded her that she can't work her way into heaven. That it's not about her good outweighing her bad."

"I see. It's just a guilty conscience, and the desire to make things right. I think you're right. I think she'll be able to stay in the house too."

"She'll be working a long time to pay the fines off, though. I've thought about helping her, but I don't think I will."

"No." He'd thought about helping her, too, but there were lessons to be learned and as hard as it was to stand back and watch someone he loved suffer, he needed to allow the consequences to be felt.

"Which reminds me, I've been thinking about this for several weeks, but I wanted to wait to say anything until we found out what was happening with Macy. Now that we know the fines and the house arrest and the probation and community service hours, and we know that she's not going anywhere for an actual prison sentence, I feel like I can ask."

"Yes?" Zoriah said, turning toward him, and slowing her steps a little.

He tugged her to a stop.

"Business at the shop has been going really well over the last two months, and we still have things that Miss Beverly has donated, as well as Lindy and your own things that we haven't even set out in the store. Back when you were researching this, you said there was a whole business wrapped around buying secondhand things and selling them."

"I did. There is. I had no idea."

"I thought about investing some money and buying a few lots, maybe some storage units, and starting a business that would dovetail with yours. Basically a secondhand retail shop that was all online." He swallowed, his throat tight. "What do you think?"

"I love it! I mean, you've been helping me so much in the shop, but I know that eventually you're going to have to find something —"

"I thought we could do it together. My girls, Macy, Mark, and you."

"That might be an oddly structured business."

"I wanted it to be a family business, because the other thing I wanted to talk to you about was," he reached in his pocket, and pulled out a little box while dropping to his knee.

His heart thudded against his chest, and his hands shook as he tried to open the box, and the pretty speech that he had memorized, the one where he told her how important she was to him, and how much she meant to him, and how much he loved her, completely flew out of his head.

Instead, he stammered, "Would...I...um, marry me?" he finally got out.

She gasped, and her hand went to her throat. "Yes. Of course. Oh my goodness," she said, tugging on his hand and pulling him to his feet.

"It isn't new," he said, indicating the ring in the box. "And if you don't like it, we can find something you do. But, when I saw this, it reminded me of you. And it felt perfect to me."

It really had. It was a pearl, swirled in old gold, beautiful and classy, and it reminded him of Zoriah. Someone who loved antiques, and who put a value on the things of the past, while still looking at her beautiful forevers.

"I love it!"

"It's not a diamond."

"It's better."

"I got an idea of what your size might be, and had a jeweler size it for me. We can change it if it doesn't fit," he said as he pulled the ring from the box, and held his hand out for her finger.

She put her hand on his, and that's when the tension left his body.

She'd said yes! He hadn't been sure. They'd been under so much pressure and stress, and although they worked well together, and she seemed to enjoy his company, and she seemed to enjoy kissing him as well, he hadn't been sure that she was ready to take this step.

"It fits," he said, smiling.

"It does. Perfectly. Thank you," she said, returning his smile before she stepped closer and put her arms around him.

He pulled her to him, and said, "No. Thank you."

He lowered his head, thinking that someday they would look back on this night, as it became one of their beautiful forevers.

Enjoy this preview of *Precious Memories,* just for you!

Precious Memories

Chapter One

Laura Wilson delicately dipped her tiny paintbrush into the small pool of black paint in the little container on her work desk.

For the last fifteen minutes, she had been trying to ignore the pounding music coming from overhead.

No. That was not true.

It wasn't hard for her to ignore the pounding music, which really didn't bother her. It was her grandfather's irritated scowls, muttered words, and jerky movements which had been getting worse and worse that had really been bothering her.

She shifted in her seat, holding the paintbrush still while she did.

Each piece of the handmade, handcrafted, personalized wooden doll people had to be perfectly done, with attention to the minutest detail.

It was what made her grandfather's shop in Blueberry Beach famous all over the eastern United States.

If her grandfather ever got set up online, he could be famous all over the world.

Her grandfather muttered again, growling, and stood up from his stool where he was working on carving the details of the latest miniature piece he was creating.

She was not as good of a carver as her grandfather, but she was a better painter.

The familiar heavy, lead feeling settled deep in her chest, and she fought the temptation to lay her head on her desk.

The exhaustion that she'd been fighting since shortly after her husband cheated on her and left was taking hold.

Carefully cleaning her brush and putting the lid back on the small container of expensive paint, she stood wearily and looked at the clock.

Just ten AM.

Alessandra and Grace were still in school, in third and first grades respectively, and they wouldn't be home for another five hours.

It felt like the morning had already lasted forever, but no matter how short it had been in reality, Laura needed a nap.

The stress from waiting on the possible eruption from her grandfather was far worse than the thumping of the music and occasional banging on the floor. It sounded like the new tenant had his volume maxed out and was dancing with fifty of his friends directly above them.

The vibrations actually were a little bit of a problem. The work they were doing was very exact and needed to be just right.

But her grandfather had always been easily irritated and prone to eruptions. His shop, Blueberry Beach Doll Shop, might not have been the best place for her to come to rest and recover, but it was the only place she could think of. She hadn't wanted to raise her children in the city anyway, and Blueberry Beach was perfect for kids.

Her grandfather picked up a stack of papers then slammed them down with a sharp slap and another growl.

It was funny, seeing how he was almost deaf anyway, that the noise would even bother him. Half the time when she spoke with him, he didn't hear what she said, but apparently, he could hear every note of the music. Or every drumbeat, since there didn't seem to be too many notes.

She chuckled to herself as she wiped her hands down her apron, then untied it and laid it over the back of her chair.

She had trained as a classical cellist but was very grateful that she'd also taken business classes in college, graduating with a dual major, since her classical music training had never earned her a full-time wage.

It just made her a music snob. She sighed, straining her shoulders then taking a step and putting a hand on her desk.

"Grandfather?" she said, trying to infuse confidence in her voice.

When she was younger, he could intimidate her. Now that she was older...he still could. But she tried to pretend he couldn't.

Her grandfather grunted. She took that as a, "What?" and continued. "I'm going to go upstairs and speak to your new tenant. I'm sure he doesn't realize how his music carries."

She hadn't actually seen the new tenant. Her grandfather had taken care of signing the lease and all that while she had been busy with her children a week ago.

She hadn't been out much, because of her exhaustion, and the man had managed to move in without her ever running into him.

She did know that it was a man, because of what her grandfather said, and she assumed he was an older gentleman, with no children, although she couldn't specifically remember Grandfather saying that.

If she had all of her old energy, she would have been in touch with her friends here in Blueberry Beach, especially Anitra and Zoriah, when she'd moved back to town. As it was, she hadn't even made it to the diner.

"He's going to get kicked out if he doesn't keep that stuff turned down. How's a man supposed to work when he can't hear himself think!" her grandfather said roughly, his irritation obvious in his choppy movements and the set of his bristled jaw.

"I'm sure he doesn't mean to, Grandfather," Laura said, unwilling to agree to repeat her grandfather's words to the man upstairs.

A particularly loud thump echoed through the small store. Just after that, the bell above the door rang, announcing customers.

Her grandfather turned toward the doorway that led into the shop showroom, which was quite small although beautifully arranged.

Normally, her grandfather was very nice and an actual grandfatherly type, and she always appreciated his words of wisdom, of which he had many.

But when he was irritated, like he was now, his temper seemed to be something he couldn't control.

"I need to see to the customers," Grandfather said, his words slightly modulated as he seemed to gather himself and put on his salesman persona before heading toward the front doorway while Laura turned toward the back.

Her grandfather had been very patient with her exhaustion and her constant need for naps and the fact that she didn't put in a full eight hours every day. More like four.

Of course, he could double his output now that she was here since she could do almost everything he could. The position she filled wasn't one that just anyone could do, although in the summer, he could often get art students from college to do some of the less detailed work.

Often, he had out-of-work artists working for him, but an artist couldn't really make a living in Blueberry Beach, and they soon left.

Laura moved down the hallway toward the back stairs. She and her grandfather lived behind the shop, where he had a kitchen, dining room, and living area, plus the upstairs which was separated into three bedrooms on one side and the tiny, two-bedroom apartment she was going to visit now on the other. The quarters were small and cramped, and if she was going to stay in Blueberry Beach, she really should find a place of her own.

She couldn't think about that, because she had no idea what she was going to do and no energy to try to come up with something.

Pausing at the bottom of the steps to take several breaths and to tell herself that she could do it, she tried to push aside the exhaustion that made her limbs feel like lead and her body feel like standing alone took superhuman effort.

The idea of climbing the stairs was almost too much. She closed her eyes and said a quick prayer, and then lifted her foot and focused on taking one step at a time. She was out of breath by the second step, but she made it to the top.

Doctors had not been able to figure out what was wrong with her and had finally just diagnosed stress.

Having her husband cheat and leave, then losing her job and severe worry about the custody of her kids—which had turned out to be for naught—had emotionally devastated her, and she supposed what she was experiencing was a nervous breakdown in old-fashioned language.

The doctors had simply advised her to rest and keep her life as stress-free as possible.

She'd also tried to eat healthy and do something normal, even if it was working for her grandfather. At least she was working. At least with Grandfather, she could pretty much set her own hours.

Reaching the top of the stairs, she stood on the landing, giving herself a minute to catch her breath.

She didn't wait long before knocking on the door. The sooner she got this over with, the sooner she could go lie down.

Not that she was sleepy, and she probably wouldn't sleep. She was just...exhausted.

She had to knock three times before the music abruptly shut off, and shortly after that, the door yanked open.

Wherever she'd gotten the idea that the new tenant was an older gentleman had been wrong.

That was her first thought as a large, athletic-looking man scowled down at her.

His t-shirt bulged over a big chest and biceps, and his tanned face held a sheen of sweat. His athletic shorts stopped at his knees, revealing firm calves. He wore the fanciest-looking athletic shoes she'd ever seen.

He was the kind of man she'd always tried to avoid, and he was just her age if she was any judge.

There might have been a little bit of gray at his temples, and his face looked weatherworn, his eyes wise if surprised and slightly narrowed, as though wondering what in the world would make her interrupt him.

Of course, avoiding this kind of man and marrying Christian, her ex, who was the opposite of everything this man was, hadn't worked out too well for her, either.

Christian had been shy and serious with a distinct lack of confidence. Laura had been attracted to him, she had to admit, mostly because of the fact that no one else would be. She wouldn't have to worry about sharing or about him leaving her or not appreciating her.

Of course, when she'd helped him build his business, and he'd become extremely successful, all that had changed, and he'd been pretty quick to find other women who would stroke his ego and do his work, and eventually, he'd dropped Laura.

Loyalty. She should have looked for a man with loyalty.

Maybe that made her wiser, but it didn't make her any more eager to jump back into a relationship with anyone.

She put everything she had into her marriage and into the business they built together, where basically they'd developed ways for people to pay vendors online and sold software that went along with that. They'd made a lot of money, but she'd been blind to the fact that her husband had become less like the man she married and more like the men she had avoided for the very reason of what had happened to her.

Never again.

Pick up your copy of *Precious Memories* by Jessie Gussman today!

A Gift from Jessie

View this code through your smart phone camera to be taken to a page where you can download a FREE ebook when you sign up to get updates from Jessie Gussman! Find out why people say, "Jessie's is the only newsletter I open and read" and "You make my day brighter. Love, love, love reading your newsletters. I don't know where you find time to write books. You are so busy living life. A true blessing." and "I know from now on that I can't be drinking my morning coffee while reading your newsletter – I laughed so hard I sprayed it out all over the table!"

Claim your free book from Jessie!

Escape to more faith-filled romance series by Jessie Gussman!

The Complete Sweet Water, North Dakota Reading Order:
Series One: Sweet Water Ranch Western Cowboy Romance (11 book series)
Series Two: Coming Home to North Dakota (12 book series)
Series Three: Flyboys of Sweet Briar Ranch in North Dakota (13 book series)
Series Four: Sweet View Ranch Western Cowboy Romance (10 book series)
Spinoffs and More! Additional Series You'll Love:
Jessie's First Series: Sweet Haven Farm (4 book series)
Small-Town Romance: The Baxter Boys (5 book series)
Bad-Boy Sweet Romance: Richmond Rebels Sweet Romance (3 book series)
Sweet Water Spinoff: Cowboy Crossing (9 book series)
Holiday Romance: Cowboy Mountain Christmas (6 book series)
Small Town Romantic Comedy: Good Grief, Idaho (5 book series)
True Stories from Jessie's Farm: Stories from Jessie Gussman's Newsletter (3 book series)
Reader-Favorite! Sweet Beach Romance: Blueberry Beach (8 book series)
Cowboy Mountain Christmas Spinoff: A Heartland Cowboy Christmas (9 book series)
Blueberry Beach Spinoff: Strawberry Sands (10 book series)

www.ingramcontent.com/pod-product-compliance
Lightning Source LLC
Chambersburg PA
CBHW070514200726
48293CB00007B/2526